Praise for *The Territory*

'Gripping dystopia with a keen po

Winner of the Gateshead YA Book

Shortlisted for the Trinity Schools Book Award

'This is a truly exceptional novel, exciting, gripping and intense, with relatable protagonists whose agonies become the reader's own. It deals with complex moral dilemmas regarding loyalty, self-preservation and family, forcing the reader to answer the uncomfortable question: who deserves to live when spaces are limited? This is the first of a trilogy and the final cliff-hanger will leave you clamouring for more.'

Book Trust

'Truly heart-wrenching! Govett raises issues about our education system, the environment and decisions governments around the world are making. I'd go so far as to call this the 1984 of our time and recommend this as a great read, with a fantastic political context.'

The Guardian children's books site

'Govett has created a powerful and shocking novel that makes the reader wonder how societies would deal with the environmental consequences of climate change and if there could ever be any 'right' course of action ... an excellent, thought-provoking book.'

Children's Books Ireland

'...an enjoyable, fast-paced read, and raises some interesting questions about how you would behave in difficult situations, as well as being a clear indictment of the UK education system...'

Books for Keeps

'The Territory is a terrific book. It simply is.'

Bookwitch

'I loved every second of this book; it was phenomenal.'

Yourbestbookpal

Sarah Govett graduated with a First in Law from Oxford University. After qualifying as a solicitor, she set up her own tutoring agency, Govett Tutors, which specialises in helping children from all backgrounds prepare for exams. Sarah has also written for children's television.

The first instalment of her award-winning debut trilogy, *The Territory*, launched in May 2015 and was followed by the second book, *The Territory, Escape*, in October 2016.

The critically acclaimed *The Territory* was shortlisted for *The Times* Chicken House Children's Fiction Prize, won the Gateshead YA Book Prize in January 2017 and has been shortlisted for the Trinity Schools Book Award 2018. Both books are included in Book Trust's recommended reads.

In addition to speaking at schools across the UK, Sarah has appeared at the Southbank Literature Festival, the Barnes Children's Literature Festival, The Edinburgh International Book Festival, the Bradford Literature Festival and the Godolphin Literary Festival. She is also a regular contributor to The Huffington Post.

Sarah lives in London with her husband and two young children.

THE TERRITORY, TRUTH

First published in 2018
by Firefly Press
25 Gabalfa Road, Llandaff North, Cardiff, CF14 2JJ
www.fireflypress.co.uk

Text © Sarah Govett 2018

A CIP catalogue record of this book is available from the British Library.

Print ISBN 978-1-910080-70-2
epub ISBN 978-1-910080-71-9

This book has been published with the support of the Welsh Books Council.

Typeset by: Elaine Sharples

Printed by Pulsio SARL

THE
TERRITORY,
TRUTH

SARAH GOVETT

For Noa and Alba

People need things to do. A focus. They can't just sit around, inert. Dad once said they'd done experiments on it. Psychological ones. People who were left in a room with nothing but a table, a chair and an electric-shock machine would choose to zap themselves with an electric current rather than remain seated and bored. Zap – ow! Zap – agggggghhhh! Over and over until the door opened again. At the time I didn't understand it. I thought, well, those are probably the results you get if you experiment on the sort of freaks who volunteer to take part in psychological experiments. But now it's starting to make sense.

A sense of purpose, a mission, is an incredible thing. It lengthens your stride, fuels your weary muscles and irons the creases out of your forehead. Today we kept walking till the sun had disappeared below the horizon and the sky was a dark pink and indigo chromatography experiment. We've settled into a pattern, a rhythm. A line of us in single file, as the drier routes are often ridges projecting out of the salt marsh below like the spine of an open book. Lee's normally at the front; me, Raf and Ella in the middle; with Nell, a ghostly white-haired fourth shadow, attached to our heels. Jack follows behind at a distance.

Lee has sort of become our unofficial leader since Megan's death. Partly because he'd been planning with Adnan back at the Fort to overthrow the Ministry for the longest. But mainly because he's the only one with the computer skills, the only one who has any hope of hacking the Ministry servers and altering the uploads. Freeing the brainwashed minds of the freakoid Childes back in the Territory and awakening them to the fact that it's A-not-OK to send tens of thousands of teens to their deaths each year just for failing to get the required 70 per cent in the TAA exam. That Norms aren't lesser beings just because they don't get to upload facts straight into their brains. That the Ministry doesn't deserve unquestioning devotion and maybe, just maybe, that fighting back against a regime that's constantly lied to you, and ending the whole TAA system could be a good thing.

Well, that's the idea anyway.

Lee's taking his new role very seriously – lots of compass-consulting and agonising over driest route versus fastest route. Occasionally though, under the shock of dark hair, his smile still breaks through – so wide it makes the gap between his front teeth seem almost normal size.

I've been alternating my time between Ella and Raf. It's so good to have Ella back in my life again – to share stuff with, to confide in. There's no BS to her. What you see is what you get. No dancing around. Sometimes, though, you see the darkness descend – if someone mentions Raiders, even in the sense of 'at least we don't need to watch our backs all the time now the Raiders are gone' – the shutters are all flipped closed and she kind of crumples in on herself. I think having Nell to look after has both helped her and also pushed the damage deeper. Ella's had to be so strong, to screen Nell from the evil that was going on around them – the Raiders' breeding programme. She's had to internalise it all. But I think she's going to get past it. Find the light again.

Raf's still pretty weak, but it's easy to forget it. The glow has returned to his face. The fire. OK, sure, his eyes have always been amazing, but now it's like they've got their own little green and blue LEDs planted in the irises. I can't quite believe that only a few days ago he was lying unconscious on the floor. *THUD* – the sound of his skull hitting the stone as the psycho Raider knocked him down. Lee said that any serious damage, brain damage, might not be immediately obvious. Might *present itself later*. Doctor-speak designed to reassure but that actually makes your skin feel like you're walking through hundreds of spiders' webs. He said that shards of bone could conceivably still be working their way deeper inside, knifing his brain tissue. That pools of blood could be collecting inside his head, applying 'pressure to the brain' that could only be relieved by an operation. A proper in-a-Ministry-hospital-with-Ministry-surgeons-in-Ministry-white-coats operation. Every time I look at Raf a tiny voice in my head whispers 'shard' and 'pool' and I'm sure he can tell as then he'll come out with, 'Don't look at me like that Noa. I'm Raf the strong! Raf the powerful!' and then he'll push his arms forward and do these exaggerated bicep flexes – which are all the more hilarious as he doesn't have hugely bigger muscles than me – and he'll pick me up and kiss me, really kiss me, as if to prove a point.

The whole day Jack remained fifty or so paces behind, still lost in his thoughts and we left him to them. We didn't need to ask what was troubling him, of course. His grief over Megan was painted on his face and written in his hunched-over gait. No amount of telling him it was going to be OK, that we'd never forget her, or her sacrifice in leading us in battle against the Raiders, was going to change anything. When you lose someone it doesn't matter that they were a war hero and a leader of the Opposition in the Wetlands, all that matters is they're gone. We just have to hope that time being a 'great healer' is true and not some malc saying that people tell other people to fob them off and move them on. Part of me wanted to slow my step. To wait for him and hold him, to hug away his pain. But I knew I couldn't. It'd be more for my benefit than his. I know Jack's over me now, so I'd just be needlessly stirring things up, antagonising Raf and resurrecting old jealousies.

We covered more distance in the afternoon than in the morning. At first we'd stopped for rests regularly, at least every hour. I'd worried about Ella and Nell's stamina. Being held captive and chained for weeks and only seeing daylight for half an hour or so a day has got to take its toll on your body. Not to mention the stress, the mental torture. I'd imagined their muscles would have wasted, like when someone breaks their arm and has it in plaster for weeks and when the plaster finally comes off you're like *what's that freaky skinny left arm doing hanging there like a straw?* But they were surprisingly strong: resilient. And I guess that every step towards the Fence was a step away from their old prison, a step towards a future that they could control.

Dinner was dried meat around a fire. Caveman-style. We ate in semi-silence, focusing on the flames. Night time is the hardest. Hope often sets with the sun and then doubts and memories rise up and haunt us. I think of Mum and Dad and worry. Worry about what's happened to them as a result of me and Raf disappearing off into the Wetlands to rescue Jack. We were meant to be at Greenhaven, starting the next step in our education, not trapped on the other side of an electric fence. Were they sitting at home, worried sick about me? Or, the unthinkable alternative, were they in some Ministry prison being questioned? Questioned, like Aunty Vicki had been? An echo of Mum's voice rang in my ears. Her guttural sobs. *She didn't survive questioning.* Should I have told them where I was going? Confessed that Jack's being shipped off was all my fault? If he hadn't overheard me choose Raf over him then he wouldn't have tried to escape before the results of the TAA came in. His 71 per cent would have counted and the three of us would have stayed safe and dry. It was my responsibility to bring him back. Mum and Dad would have understood, surely? Understood that I'd just lost Daisy to a botched late-upgrade – a failed attempt to turn her into a freakoid Childe that had instead reduced her to a vegetable. One they'd disposed of. Understood that I couldn't lose my other best friend as well.

Then I think about our plan and all the holes in it. The gaps. Like how were we going to find out when our bit of the Fence was turned off for circuit testing so we could get through it without being fried? And was Lee even right that these circuit tests happened?

Thoughts, thoughts, thoughts.

The kind that scramble your brain until you get lost in them. Sirens calling you into the fog, towards the rocks. I had to resist them. We all did. Force our minds back to the flames. Concentrate instead on the crackle and the spit and the way the light changed as larger flames rose and ate the smaller ones above. It probably helped that we were partially intoxicated by the extreme amounts of mosquito repellent that all of us except Nell had applied. Her Cell skin and blood, the result of the same mutation that made her hair ghostly white, was protection enough against the lethal breed of mosquitoes that haunted the Wetlands.

Raf sat next to me and I nuzzled into him.

'We're going to do this, aren't we?' I asked quietly, trying to still the tremor in my voice. 'Get through the Fence? Bring down the system?'

He didn't answer immediately. Just leaned closer and stared into my eyes, stared like he was gazing all the way down into my soul.

'Yes, Noa. Yes, we are.'

I used to think that shooting stars were stars dying in galaxies far away, falling out of the sky – their golden trails a kind of farewell bow. Adieu universe. Granting wishes as their departing gift.

Then we studied them at school and found out that they weren't actually stars at all – they were meteorites –

small bits of rock burning up from friction as they entered the Earth's atmosphere. Less romantic. More true.

There was an incredible shooting star last night. I woke up – no idea when. It was nowhere near morning but you could still make out the contours of the land, the huddled bundles of our sleeping group and the surrounding shrubby trees as the moon was a full-on circle – a massive eco bulb in the sky. I'd been having a horrific dream, a nightmare about Mum. Someone had been drilling a hole in the back of her neck and forcing a Node in. She was going to be brainwashed into forgetting all about me, forgetting that she'd ever had a daughter at all, so being awake in the middle of the night was actually a major relief. An escape. I tried to calm my racing mind so I focused on the stars. The sparkling canopy above us. Thinking, you count sheep to relax, right? So why not stars? I began to count. *One, two, three* … and that's when it hit, or rather fell. Well, not on three to be honest, because that would be far too convenient. Nothing ever happens on the count of three apart from a magic trick. Hey presto. No, it was on more like twenty-seven, not that it matters. What does matter is that suddenly, out of nowhere, there was this burning streak across the sky, ripping it apart. It was so huge and seemed so close that at one point I started freaking out that it might land right on top of us and we'd be crushed to death by a burning fireball.

It didn't. We weren't. It must have crashed into the ground some miles away, or maybe hundreds of miles away. Distance can be difficult to judge, especially at night. The stars don't exactly look like they'd take more than a lifetime of space travel to reach.

When morning came, I didn't tell anyone about it. I don't know why. It's not like I'd been planning to keep it secret. But there was something special about the moment. Watching it fall. When it seemed like it was just the star/meteorite, the moon and me.

The three of us awake, alone in the world.

We've been walking for three days now and already most of the streams are sweet. The animals are starting to drink from them. Jack was the first to notice. He's always had a special connection to animals, an affinity if you like. Rex, my dog from back then, was normally wary of people outside the family, but he'd always roll over for Jack. Expose his vulnerable belly and then slobber all over Jack's hand.

We were rounding the bend of a stream when Jack suddenly held his hand up, flat, a teacher calling a class to attention, and then pressed it to his lips. The signal was clear. Stop. Silence. There, up ahead, was the most beautiful animal I've ever seen. A deer. A real live deer, a history book brought to life. With these huge brown eyes, soulful and sad – the sort of eyes I've always imagined Aslan would have as he's telling Lucy there's a way to get Edmund back but he knows what sacrifice it's going to involve. The deer bent its graceful neck to drink from the stream and then, probably sensing us, took off in ballerina leaps across the marram grass.

'Fresh water!' I murmured and looked round to see other lips moving too, the discovery so wonderful it had to be vocalised. As one, we bounced towards the stream, plunging in hands, lapping from open palms. Nell started laughing and then we were all joining in. Laughing with joy at an environment that could actually sustain us. I felt like an ancient explorer – this land is good, let's settle here (minus the let's plant a flag and massacre all the people who look a bit different and already live here bit).

We haven't come across a mosquito swarm yet, touch wood. I can spot them now. We all can. There was one yesterday, to the east, a small dense, low cloud in an otherwise clear sky. We could hear it, hear their evil cry – ehehehehehehehehe – but it veered off towards the salt flats and never came close.

There are more animals everywhere now. Not just deer, but rabbits, mice, even foxes scampering into bushes, fleeing into the long grass as they register our approach. Raf tried to catch us a rabbit for breakfast and failed just as dismally as on our journey into the Wetlands. Back when we were looking for Jack. It seems like a lifetime ago. Once again I had to fight down the laughter that bubbled up as he face-planted into a sandy mound, empty hands stretched out in front of him, like someone miming scoring a try in rugby. He tried to shrug it off, but I can tell it bothers him, properly bothers him that he hasn't caught anything yet.

'Maybe just leave it,' I suggested. 'Hunting's clearly not your thing.'

A mistake. Never be that honest. Guys' egos just can't handle it. His eyes went flat.

'I did catch that seagull, remember? When we were totally dehydrated and we thought we wouldn't make it. I killed that seagull.'

I told my face to agree, to 'be supportive', but my eyebrow disobeyed my brain's command and shot up in an exaggerated gesture of 'oh yeah?' A split second and then Raf had the good grace to grin.

'OK. I accept the seagull couldn't fly at the time. But if you ever need someone to pick up a dead or injured bird for you, I'm your guy!'

At least Raf doesn't take himself too seriously for too long and I think everything would have remained all happy and jokey if then, at that exact moment, Jack hadn't sauntered up carrying a couple of ducks that he'd caught in some snare he'd set before bed.

Raf walked off.

He didn't say anything, but that's the thing. When something bothers him he never does.

The helicopter came in the morning.

We were packing up after breakfast and stamping out the last embers of the fire when we heard the thuck-whop-thuck of its rotary blades slicing the air. I'd only ever seen one in a photo, only ever heard one in a sound-file clip. Freaky, menacing creatures that looked like they'd been invented by a scientist who'd managed to splice some wasp DNA into a machine.

The Ministry.

It had to be. No one else had helicopters.

They'd found us.

My stomach shrank to a tight knot and the breath caught in my throat. Trapped. I'd known this moment would come, the showdown inevitable. But I'd thought it'd be on the other side of the Fence. That we were safe from their reach here.

We all instinctively dropped to the floor, bellies touching earth, and swivelled our necks in the direction of the noise. Yoga pose for *Totally Screwed*. The sound waves were an advance party – the helicopter itself was still only a black speck on the horizon. If you chose to, you could even have pretended it was a toy. That there was a kid out there somewhere with a remote control, playing at being a pilot.

There was no time to pretend.

Lee was first to spring into action.

'Grab everything. Hurry. To the bushes.'

No one minded the commands. Authority, in itself, was comforting. Someone was in charge. Someone would protect us. We scrambled up, filling and grabbing bags, untying mosquito nets, staying low, a cluster of crabs in convoy to the protection offered by a low row of bramble bushes. We squatted behind them but it wasn't going to be cover enough. We had to get under them, inside.

Biting back a scream as thorns claimed flesh, I led the way, crawling underneath the central bush, only stopping when I was as far under as I could go. Ella, Nell, Raf and Lee followed. Soon all of us were crouched in a line, watching events unfold through a network of snaking green stems.

Then it struck me – there were only five of us. Where was Jack?

Thuck-whop, thuck-whop. The sound was growing louder and louder. I scanned left and right. A kilometre or so away the trees and bushes were already starting to bend and wave wildly, caught in the air currents.

I spotted him. Jack. At the camp, crouched by the fire.

'Come on!' I called.

If he heard, he didn't register.

The sand around him began to rise and dance.

'*Jack!*' This time I was screaming.

I made to go after him, but Raf pulled me back. 'They'll see you.'

Ella's arm was tightly wrapped round Nell's thin frame, the other hand reached up to her face. It had red marks on it where she'd been gnawing at the knuckles. Nell wasn't saying anything, no words at least. Her face was hidden in Ella's top and she was making this tiny low-pitched humming noise. Like a faulty dimmer switch.

'How do they know we're here?' whispered Ella, the whites of her eyes magnified by fear.

'I don't know,' Lee whispered back. 'It makes no sense.'

Maybe they'd noticed all the fires – the settlements left burning by the Raiders, I thought. Maybe they'd come to investigate. Or maybe – a horrific thought burrowed into my brain – maybe Megan hadn't been paranoid when she'd accused me and Raf of being spies. She'd just accused the wrong people. Maybe there *was* a spy at the Fort. A spy who'd fed our plans back to the Ministry. Which was now coming to wipe us out.

Thuck-whop, thuck-whop. The helicopter came closer and closer, making the cells in our bodies vibrate, dancing to its tune.

I couldn't take it anymore. Jack was still out there. I

closed my eyes. I think I must have stopped breathing as well, as I felt Raf's arms catch round my ribcage. I hadn't even realised I was falling.

I came round to see Jack throw himself into the bush next to me.

I punched him hard in the arm. Over and over. 'What were you thinking?'

Raf didn't even try and disguise his anger. 'If you're on some sort of suicide mission, you're doing it on your own, not taking us down with you.'

'I was scattering the fire. Burying it. So it didn't give away our position.'

'And a person, out in the open, that wouldn't?' A muscle in Raf's left cheek was beginning to twitch.

'Not now.' I managed to inject enough steel into my tone to cut them both off before it escalated any further.

Thuck-whop, thuck-whop. The sound reached maximum volume and we all instinctively flattened our bodies as much as we could. Begging the ground for sanctuary.

Then the noise receded slightly and our bodies stopped shaking quite so much. A few seconds later it stopped altogether. The helicopter had landed. Some distance away, in a dip.

'I don't get it,' Lee this time. 'Why land there? The land's flat and dry here. Why not come closer?'

'Maybe they're giving us a head start,' Jack replied. 'Maybe the sick bastards like a chase?'

We stayed frozen in position, getting weird pins and needles in cramped legs, torn between running and revealing our position or staying put and waiting for the Ministry to come and get us. We stayed put and it was the right decision. An endless hour later the helicopter rose back into the sky and flew away.

Thuck-whop, thuck-whop fading back to silence.

We found what they'd been after just as the sun was at its highest point in the sky. We were rounding a mound we'd had to detour past to continue north-west when we came across the crater. It wasn't particularly huge or deep – about the size of the pool that used to be in the middle of People's Park. The one we used to push model sailing boats about in as kids in the summer before the water went all diseased and they filled it in to make a lavender garden. Bees replacing boats.

The crater's sandy edges were patterned with footprints – Ministry boots – and off to the left was a flattened disc of earth where the helicopter must have landed. The crater itself was partly filled with water, but that wasn't anything unusual. Nothing to explain our slack jaws and bulging eyes. No, it was what lay inside the crater, what floated on the water or protruded from it, that injected adrenalin into our bloodstreams. Scattered across its diameter was a series of large, shiny metal pieces. Part of a silvery cylinder lay on its side, already the perching place for a family of ducks. To its right lay several bits of thin rectangular something that caught the sun and glinted like solar panels and behind them, directly facing us, was a huge curved dish, a pupil-less eye, staring.

'Is it?' Nell began, stuttering.

'Yes?' Ella, coaxing, patient as ever.

'Is it a UFO?' Her voice was excitement distilled.

I began to let out a laugh, when Ella touched my arm and shot me a warning glare.

'No, Nell, no I'm afraid it's not, love.'

Ella let Nell down in the gentlest of ways but still Nell's face deflated as if she'd thought that aliens were going to be the solution to all our problems. Apparently she'd heard about UFOs from one of the other Cells who had been held hostage, one who'd come from some weird cult settlement, and had fixated on them ever since. No room on Earth? Don't worry. We'll beam you up to our planet and all live in peace.

Raf had been silent, staring intently at the crater below. Finally he opened his mouth.

'It looks like a sort of communications satellite. An old one I think. Maybe a spy one. No country's been launching these for a while. Well, that's the official message anyway.'

He caught me staring at him.

'What?' He flashed me a lopsided grin. 'So, I like space. Kill me.'

It shouldn't have surprised me. Raf had this thirst for knowledge, this need to know more and to understand everything. It was this same thirst that had stopped him from uploading, made him realise the personality change that would happen if he did.

'I wonder when it fell?' Lee added. 'It would have been quite a sight. The best shooting star ever.'

His words started a memory retrieval in my brain. Click click whirr.

'Three nights ago,' I said. I explained about the unnaturally bright shooting star I'd seen that night.

Raf shot me a look. Nothing too obvious, but I could still read the disappointment in it. Disappointment that I hadn't shared something with him.

A smile attacked Lee's face.

'What is it?' I asked.

'If you're right then maybe we're not too late. Maybe some of the parts are still salvageable. Won't have rusted or been corroded by the water yet. We could use them! Communications you say, Raf?'

Raf nodded.

'This is amazing!' Lee crowed. He was totally buzzing. 'Isn't this amazing?!'

'But…' Five pairs of eyes swivelled to look at me. I hated to be the negative voice, but someone had to say it.

'If it was that important, wouldn't the Ministry people have taken it away with them?'

'Depends why they were looking,' Lee replied. 'Maybe they were checking it wasn't a missile or a spy satellite. Maybe this is one of their own. In any event, it might have something we can use that's irrelevant to them.'

'Like?'

'A transmitter.' Lee's eyes were aglow. 'Something we might be able to adapt to trigger the system controlling the Fence. Something we could use to turn a section of the Fence off!'

Knowing a big fat zero about how computers work or what a transmitter is, taking parts from a crashed satellite to hack a system that controls a massive electric fence didn't make a huge amount of sense to me, but I nodded sagely as if I totally got it all and, without any more discussion, we were all clambering down the mound and across the flat to get a closer look.

It was kind of awe inspiring seeing the pieces of metal just lying there. A satellite grave. And realising, knowing, that these not-particularly-special-looking pieces had been up there – in space – circling our world. Gazing down on Earth and viewing it as a cloudy marble. I remember when I first saw the image of Earth like that. Daisy had thought it looked beautiful, like a jewel, but I'd thought it looked so fragile and lost. Colour drowning in a sea of black.

Raf and Lee squatted by the main cylinder, Raf's hand tracing the metal as if he could absorb knowledge of the universe from it by osmosis. His brain swelling with understanding like potato tubers in a beaker of distilled water.

Jack sat down by himself at the edge of the crater, the toe of his boot kicking the sandy earth, his face a black hole, ready to suck in any joy that dared approach.

It was a shock to see him like this as he's been becoming himself again. He's been walking as part of the group, and talking again. Not loads or anything, but then he was never what you'd call a chatty guy. And he's let his sweetness shine through again. Slowly lowering the barriers. Nell was tired for the last stretch of yesterday's walk and Jack caught her up and swung her onto his shoulders. Her thin, ghostly white legs dangling down, beating a soft rhythm against his chest. She had this massive grin, like a little girl whose normally workaholic dad has finally pulled a sickie for the day to play with her.

This was the Jack I knew and liked. OK, I can admit it now, loved, in a way. This was the Jack I wanted to keep. I hated seeing bitter, sad Jack. An imposter in his skin.

I decided to risk it and walked over.

'Penny for them?'

'I was just thinking how absurd it all is, you know?'

'No, but try me.'

'That we, that people, humans have achieved so much

– we've populated every country on Earth, we've explored space, we've developed crazily complex ways of spying on other countries, as if that's where the danger lay – but we couldn't do something loads simpler: we couldn't just live in a way that didn't destroy our planet, that didn't mess up everything for everyone for ever.'

I sat down by him, quiet. The satellite discovery didn't seem quite so fun anymore.

'Here, Jack, mate, I need you,' Lee's voice came from the right and shook us from our thoughts. Jack saw Lee struggling with the cylinder part of the satellite and dragged himself up and over. His strides were so long that I was always a step and a splash behind.

'See this door here?' Lee pointed to a square panel. We need to open this. It's stuck firm. If it's been welded shut in the heat of re-entry we don't stand a chance.'

Lee stood aside and Jack examined the hatch.

'It's not welded – you can see this crack. The one there – like a piece of black string? Yes, that's the one. It just needs force.'

Jack's no scientist, but he gets stuff. He's practical but in some kind of wise way. It's like he looks at things and just gets how they work. Intuitive if you like. Once when our toaster had stopped working he mended it by giving it a sharp rap on one side and then blowing on it. Seriously.

Jack wandered off for several minutes and then returned with a sharp pointed stone and a heavy rock. He held the point of the stone to the crack and then just started to hammer relentlessly with the rock. His muscles rippled and sweat poured down his forehead from exertion. I felt… No … forget what I felt.

Finally he did it, the door cracked open and Lee was free to root around inside the cylinder where all the circuitry was.

The rest of us had gathered round at a respectful distance, disciples waiting for news of a miracle.

Waiting.

We knew the moment Lee lifted his face again. Gone was the face-splitting grin and palpable excitement.

'No joy, I'm afraid,' he said, trying to keep his voice light and failing. 'We'll take the circuitry and memory chips in case we can analyse them later, but there's nothing we can use now. The electronics have all short circuited in the water.'

Some things are only scary if you let them be. They only have power by association. Like the hoverfly in wasp's clothing. Or the rope round an adult elephant's foot that can't actually restrain the animal, the elephant just thinks it can as it held it back as a baby.

The Fence is nothing like this. It isn't just a symbol. It's designed to keep us out. To kill. And it's never failed. Of all the hundreds and thousands of people who've been shipped off to the Wetlands, there's not one known case of someone making it back.

I gagged as I remembered standing at the end of the path near Aunty Vicki's house, watching as a skeletal woman attempted to scale the Fence with her son. She was shaking as the electricity coursed through her, an epileptic puppet. And then came the sweet smell of cooking meat. Her boy's hand never reached the Fence, but the automated machine guns made his body dance inches from the wire.

Seeing the Fence for third time didn't make it any less horrifying. We approached it just before dusk. A thick fog was swirling in from the sea, clinging to our ankles and turning the air opaque. The sort of evening you'd never enter a graveyard even if you didn't believe in ghosts, because it'd make you realise that a tiny bit of your brain wasn't so sure.

Rising out of the fog, higher and higher, the Fence climbed skyward – a floodlit towering electrified web with the mosquito grids above. An eerie glowing line across the horizon, punctuated at regular intervals by the dark shapes of the motion-detector machine-gun towers. They say you can see the Great Wall of China from space. If that's true you must be able to see the Fence too. I wonder what it'd look like? A pale scratch across the land.

It must have been a trick of the eye caused by the spiralling fog, but the Fence seemed to pulse slightly. As if it were living. Breathing. Waiting. For us.

No one spoke. Everyone lost in their own private nightmare. Well, everyone apart from Nell, who started to whimper quietly into the folds of Ella's clothes. It hit me – she'd been born out here. Deep in the Wetlands. She'd never have seen the Fence before and had had no clue what we were up against. I wanted to protect her from it. To turn her head and wipe the image but I didn't know how. Luckily someone else did.

'I don't know about anyone else, but I'm starving!' Jack spoke with exaggerated enthusiasm, spinning Nell up on to his shoulders, pointing her away from the horror. Ella mouthed her thanks but Jack didn't see, he was already off in the other direction.

'Let's go catch some food!' he called and started galloping back to camp, bouncing Nell around until she stopped crying and, instead, muffled peals of laughter floated back towards us.

We've set up camp about a mile away from the Fence. We couldn't risk our base being any closer, not knowing what the Ministry has here in terms of surveillance. Not knowing if any of the machine-gun towers are actually manned. And, anyway, the land ahead of us is pock-marked with craters, an acne casualty of bombing designed to destroy any houses that had been near the Fence, to prevent any Fish, the poor souls living here, setting up home or massing at the border.

With the transmitter option raised and dashed we're back to Lee's original plan. Sure the logic is sound(ish): the Fence is too long to be electrified on a single circuit. It must be broken into sections, each on their own circuit. Sections that need to be tested independently to check that they're still working. And, during these tests, one section of the Fence won't be live – the sensors won't be working. It will be reduced to a high wire wall that we can cut our way through.

'So?' Jack asked, as we were draping mosquito nets over stick frames. 'How do we know if the Fence is on or not?'

This was it. The biggie.

Lee paused and looked up, not quite meeting anyone's eye.

'Well, if it's live, it will fr … electrocute … objects.'

'Objects?' Me this time. Lee was swallowing his words and dancing round the issue. I wanted to pin him down.

'Creatures,' he clarified, quietly.

'No.' Ella's voice was firm. A resounding gong sound. Come in from the playground now or you're in serious trouble. 'You're not actually suggesting that we're going to hurl small animals at the Fence to see if they fry?'

Lee just swallowed again and said nothing. He had clearly been suggesting just that. A vision of a rabbit shaking and cooking on the wire attacked my head and left me feeling a bit sick.

'We eat animals anyway,' Raf weighed in on Lee's side. 'All of us. This isn't different. And wouldn't you prefer to sacrifice a few rabbits and mice than risk us frying? Failing in the mission that we've been entrusted with? Letting the Ministry continue as it is?'

'This is different.' I wasn't on Raf's side and this made me uncomfortable, but I had to speak my mind. I don't know exactly why, but using animals as circuit testers seemed very different from eating them.

Jack opened his mouth and I thought, this is going to get ugly, everyone joining in, no agreement reached, but then I heard what he had to say.

'I'm obviously not the science brain here, probably the least so, but surely animals aren't the only things that conduct electricity? In experiments at school we weren't exactly linking rabbits up to crocodile clips, we were using metal.'

We were all listening. All we could hear was Jack's voice and the gentle burble of the nearby stream.

'Well,' Jack continued, 'all the settlements have metal things in their walls, and shacks made from corrugated iron, which they've clearly taken from stuff lying around, stuff from the old houses. Why can't we just get bits of metal to throw at the Fence?'

I felt embarrassed not to have thought of this myself. Lee and Raf, too, judging by their semi-flushed faces that the not particularly warm fire couldn't explain.

I smiled my thanks to Jack and Ella gave him a squeeze. He didn't say anything but he was clearly chuffed. Pleased to make a contribution that went beyond being weirdly big and strong for his age.

Everyone agreed. We would search for metal. Any scrap bits we could find, bits that were small enough to throw from a distance but heavy enough to travel the distance to the Fence. We were looking for projectiles.

Tonight was my, Raf and Nell's first turn on Fence duty. We've devised a rota. The day divided into two sections. Section 1: collecting metal, food and water and sleeping; section 2: hurling bits of metal at an electrified fence. I doubt a similar timetable has ever been made up anywhere in the world, but we don't know when the Fence might be tested. We have to be ready. Ella split us into the two groups. I was surprised when she suggested that Nell went with me and Raf rather than her and when she chose Jack and Lee. But it made sense in a way. She knows Nell needs to increase her confidence, knows that with what we're attempting, there might be a time when

Ella's not there for her. Not there full stop. And Ella doesn't seem to want to be teamed up with Raf herself. Not in any way that she shows outright and certainly not in anything that she's said, but she seems to engineer it that she's never sat next to him, never doing the same task at exactly the same time. And she doesn't laugh at his jokes in the way that she laughs with Jack and Lee. I think it's the freakoid thing. He's the first Childe she's properly met and she's still suspicious and can't get over it. Past it. The Node is all she sees.

As everyone else snuggled down for the night, me and Raf pulled on massively heavy backpacks – metal isn't exactly light – and slow-footed it off to the west. We'd discussed camouflaging ourselves in case there was anyone in a tower watching but in the end we rejected the idea. It was the sight of Raf holding a branch in front of his face that sealed the deal. You could totally see all his features through the twigs and all it did was make him look like a terrible 'Christmas Tree Number 3' from a school play.

Nell trotted at my side, her pack considerably lighter, her nimble leaps showing up my graceless thumps. Raf made to hold my hand, but I moved away. It didn't seem massively appropriate with Nell there too and, as much as I craved the comfort, the lizard part of my brain knew I shouldn't relax, that comfort was the enemy. My senses were firing on high alert and I needed to listen to them.

The night was colder than normal and a thick fog was

rolling in again, swirling round our feet, turning the landscape dreamlike and surreal. Like someone had carried out a guerrilla attack with a smoke machine as part of a performance art project. Performance art is a bit malc. It almost makes me appreciate why they introduced scale drawings instead. Almost. If the Fence hadn't been floodlit, we wouldn't have had a clue which way to go as the dark made reading the compass pretty impossible even when screwing up my face into weird squint eye expressions. We had reed torches we could light for the return, but they took some time to make and we didn't want to use them when we didn't totally have to.

We stumbled into craters and over brambles. One particularly vicious thorn tore a chunk from my thigh, Nell stumbled over a molehill and Raf strode through a puddle that only looked about a centimetre deep but turned out to be a mini plunge pool.

Wet and scratched, we arrived at our destination – a patch of wild, scrappy bushes – prime Fence-watching space, just this side of the floodlit zone. Beyond the bushes was a fast-flowing stream, more of a river actually, and then, about three road widths' further, stood the Fence itself. I didn't need to look at Nell to know that she was shaking. We all were. I was thirsty so I dipped my finger into the river. A distraction. There was that lingering taste that catches at the back of your throat. Salt. We'd have to make our water bottles last.

The lights were bright. Even brighter than before, it seemed, but maybe it was just that my eyes hadn't seen electricity for over a month. Had got used to the gentler illumination of fire and sun. I blinked. Blinked again. Pupils reacting and constricting.

'Are you sure we won't trigger the guns from here?' Raf whispered.

I nodded my response. I was as certain as I could be. When I'd seen the woman attempt to scale the Fence, the guns didn't activate until she was on the wire itself and her little boy was standing next to it at her feet.

Silently, seriously, we opened our backpacks and formed a pile of metal pieces in front of us. I picked one up, cradling the cold surface in my palm, and rotated my arm forward and back again – attempting a warm-up.

I looked at Raf doing the same and started giggling. Soon Nell joined in, the tension, the sombre mood shattered. It suddenly felt like we were in a lame school PE class about to practise shot put – the most pointless of all sports. Why the Ministry still included it was beyond me. We couldn't exactly learn to hurl the infra-red rays that caused global warming back into space again.

'Right. Bet I can hit the Fence first,' I taunted.

'I'll have you know I'm excellent at Fence attack,' Raf rejoined. 'It's my specialist sport.'

'Me first,' Nell's voice, high but with a determination that caught me off guard.

She windmilled her skinny arm and then let go, sending a piece of roadsign off at a 45-degree angle. It landed in the river with a splash.

We collapsed in laughter again.

All of our first throws fell pitifully short but then we put more into it, included a run up and when my first piece hit home with a ping and a fiery burst of yellow, we broke into a manic war dance accompanied by jubilant yells and then a sudden, panicked, gulpy silence. We were densers. We weren't supposed to be drawing attention to ourselves. What if someone saw? What if the pressure of something just hitting the Fence triggered the sensors? We hit the ground and waited. Waited for the gunfire to come.

It didn't. The towers here can't be manned. The sensors can't be that strong.

Relief can be dizzying and it took a few minutes for us to pick ourselves up. We continued to take turns to throw, to test. After a while our arms tired, muscles we didn't usually use becoming over-worked. We realised we were getting through the metal scraps far too fast and we had to pace ourselves if we were going to make them last the full eight hours. It also started to sink in that the yellow sparks weren't a cause for celebration. They weren't fireworks or trophies. The opposite in fact. We wanted no sparks. No electricity. The exuberance was gone. Not to return. This was business. Survival. And we had to remember that.

We started to divide up our time. To throw a test piece every fifteen minutes and then talk the rest, eking out our food and water supplies to keep energy levels even.

Raf went all quiet for a while. He didn't say what the matter was but I could tell from the tension in his face, the slight grey of his skin, that it wasn't just the Fence getting him down. He was getting one of his headaches again. He'd had one the day before yesterday, with slightly pixilated vision, a bit like a migraine, and had to go and lie down with his eyes closed till it passed. Lee had seen my horrified expression and was quick to say it didn't necessarily mean anything. That headaches after concussion and a knock to the skull were normal, expected. But 'didn't necessarily mean anything' still meant that they might mean something. Might mean something horrific.

Pool. Shard.

I needed to distract myself so I talked to Nell, asking question after question to fill the quiet. And it was good, in a way, this time. I got to know Nell a bit, see her as an individual rather than just an appendage of Ella's.

'Do you miss it? Home, I mean. Your settlement?' I asked, eloquent and concise as ever.

'No.' Nell's response was abrupt. Definite.

I was a bit taken aback but tried to understand. I knew both her parents had died of malaria when she was a baby, but surely the rest of her settlement would have rallied round and raised her. Unless…

'Did you … were you taken really young? Before you can remember?' I ventured.

'No.' Nell hesitated. 'It wasn't like that. *They* took me at the end of last winter. Just as the snowdrops were coming out.' I'd heard that exact same *they* from Ella. She never said the word Raiders either. Just *they*, as if saying their name might risk summoning them back. Nell barked a laugh. '*They* commented on it, the flowers. How fitting they were. White flowers for white hair. It was horrible, obviously. Horrible. Not that they did what they did to Ella to me. I was too young, they said.' I gave up a silent prayer at this. 'But,' at this point Nell's voice cracked and tears ran down her cheeks, 'there were moments I was almost *grateful* to them, you know. No, no, of course you don't. Don't tell Ella I said that. Please don't tell Els. You now think I'm evil…'

I wrapped my arms round Nell's shoulders and squeezed.

'Course I don't. Tell me.'

'Well, because of them I discovered that there were others. Like me. Cells. That I wasn't alone. That I wasn't … *an abomination*.'

My breath caught in my throat. An abomination? Who puts thoughts like that into little girls' heads?

'There wasn't anyone like me at my settlement. No one. No one at all.'

Between sobs it all spilt out. Nell had been born at

Ararat, a super-religious settlement over to the west. Their leader believed that the floods, the destruction of the planet, was God's punishment for a world that turned its back on faith. His new community would follow a different path. The True Path. Everything, every part of Nell's day had been ritual, prayer and, for her, abuse. The mental kind. With her white hair and chalk-white skin Nell was seen as an ungodly freak, an abomination. The fact that no mosquito ever so much as touched her only compounded their suspicion. She must be in league with Lucifer. No wonder she wanted to stay with Ella rather than go back. How she can still smile, still retain any scrap of innocence is incredible, way more miraculous even than her skin.

We talked and threw until the premonition of dawn sent the birds into chorus and the rabbits scurrying into the open.

Raf had recovered by now and was so keen to show me he was OK that he demanded to throw the last missile. We sent up a collective prayer. Don't spark this time. Be off. Please, Fence, be off.

But the Fence paid us no heed and the metal landed with a clang and a bright orange flash.

It was freakishly hot today. There's all that stuff in books and plays about temperature influencing moods, about there being links between heat and aggression. I mean, if you think about it, the words temper and temperature must have the same roots in whatever language they came from, Latin probably. Anyway, I for one totally buy it.

Lee, Jack and Ella returned to base camp at midday, under their very own thundercloud.

'We didn't expect you till dark?' I said, wary of Lee's flashing eyes and Jack's scowl.

Jack and Lee didn't respond, just stomped off in opposite directions, so I latched on to Ella instead.

'What's going on?'

'It's not working,' she replied. 'Lee's plan's not working. We've been throwing bits of metal at the Fence for three days now and there's no change – no sign that there'll ever be a change. Jack pointed this out to Lee in a none-too-tactful way and Lee took it really badly and got all defensive and angry.'

As if on cue I heard Lee's shouted reply to something Jack must have said.

'What do you suggest, then, art boy? That we *draw* ourselves out of the situation?'

This was getting out of control. Someone was going to

go too far. Say something that couldn't be taken back. An invisible line crossed.

'Come on, guys!' Raf stood up from where he'd been skinning a rabbit and raised his voice. 'Group meeting, now.'

Everyone obeyed, as if they'd secretly wanted a referee to rock up and end things.

We gathered round the now-cold fire pit and strips of dried meat and bottles of water were passed from hand to hand like a ritual peace offering.

No one was speaking so I started.

'Lee,' I made my voice as gentle as possible, trying to channel Dad who always managed to soothe Mum when she'd had some crazy stressful time at work. 'In a way, Jack does have a point. The plan doesn't seem to be working.'

'It might,' he responded, with no trace of the manic smile I liked so much. His black eyebrows were knitted tight together, approaching monobrow status. 'We haven't given it long enough.'

'It's been three days,' Jack interjected, with no attempt at softness.

Silence.

'I've been thinking,' I began again. How to phrase this without causing further conflict? 'That our plan might be too flawed.'

Lee's mouth was a thin line but there was a vulnerability to his eyes. He was listening.

'We can't continuously throw objects at the Fence. There are gaps between throws, intervals. Not to mention the time when groups are changing over. We've been acting like the circuit will be down for at least an hour, but a circuit test might just last a few seconds, mightn't it? Or less even. Off for a miniscule amount and then straight back up again?'

I wanted Lee to interrupt, to shout me down. To tell me that circuit tests didn't work like that. That our section of Fence would be off for half a day and we just had to keep doing what we were doing.

But he didn't, shout that is. He didn't say anything. He just very slowly nodded his head.

When she was eleven, Daisy went through a stage of keeping a journal by her bed. This was when she was going through her wanting to be a writer phase. She was convinced that people were at their most creative when they were asleep and their subconscious had free rein. Her hope was that an amazing idea for a novel would pop into her dreams and then she'd wake up and write it down before she forgot it by morning. It didn't really work for her. She gave up writing stuff down after she'd had this super weird dream where she was on a date with

37

Mr Daniels(!), our horrific headmaster, and he kept on ordering peas for her and telling her she needed to remember how many peas she'd eaten as that would definitely come up in the TAA.

I don't have a journal so when my eureka moment hit in the middle of the night, I knew I had to wake someone else up and share it there and then.

My vocal functions and word sequencing took a while to catch up with my firing brain and Raf was wrenched from sleep by my tugging at his arm and triumphantly mumbling, 'Satellite … water… Ah ha!'

I waited, grinning smugly, as he came to and my speech normalised. He was giving me a slightly patronising look – *yes, love, you've had a dream, well done, now go back to sleep*. To be fair on him, the last time I'd woken like this it was because I'd dreamt talking wolves were after us, not because they wanted to eat us, but because they wanted to steal our hair and turn it into wigs.

This time, though, my dream made sense, and it was pretty damn important.

'We've been going about it all wrong – waiting for the circuit to be switched off. Waiting for something we can't control.'

'What other choice do we have?' he queried, the remnants of sleep adding these really sexy gravelly tones to his voice and turning his eyes into deep blue and green pools. 'The transmitter's not going to work, Noa. Lee said it was destroyed by the saltwater.'

'Exactly!'

'I'm not following.'

'That's what water does. Saltwater especially. It destroys electric circuits – short circuits them.'

'So?'

It's difficult sometimes explaining things. When they're so clear in your head and you don't get why the other person isn't keeping up, although you sort of appreciate it's not totally their fault as you've left out loads of stages of reasoning.

'So we use that. We short circuit the section of Fence.'

'How?'

I bit back a scream of exasperation.

'What was in front of it? What did we have to get the bits of metal over?'

Raf got it. He got it at last. And by the way his eyes went ping and his mouth went all hungry and wolfy, it can't have been a totally rubbish plan.

'The river. We divert the river. You little midnight genius.' And then he grabbed me and kissed me until Ella, woken by the noise, yelled out, 'Shut up, guys. Wait until you've got a room at least.'

The timetable's changed. No more chucking metal at the Fence. Lots more hunting and weaving instead. To dig you need spades. And if you don't have any spades you need something to trade with people who might.

I've skinned fifteen rabbits this morning. Turned beautiful furry animal after beautiful furry animal into a glistening body of muscle and sinew. Like the outside was just a lie. A cuddly toy. And the inside is the truth of existence – all raw and alien. Repetition doesn't make it OK. It's still horrible. Still makes my stomach contract and shiver. But you get used to it after a while. More used to it, anyway.

We stopped at twenty. Like we were in the Bible or something. *A score of rabbits and two score of reed torches.*

Me and Raf are on trading duty. Nell's drying more reeds and plaiting them into torches so when the time comes we can keep travelling by night. Lee and Ella are working out which bit of the river is going to be the easiest to divert and Jack's going to be our resident beaver and collect logs, the biggest he can carry, for when we get to the damming stage.

Ella took a bit of convincing to get on board with the new plan. OK most of the others did to be fair.

'If water can turn the Fence off then how come it's not

down every time it rains? Why isn't it shorted all the time by the water on the ground?'

I dug into my brain's store of chemistry facts leftover from the TAA and launched into an explanation about rainwater being reasonably pure and how you need the impurities in the saltwater; and then went into how there might be the occasional puddle near the Fence but the Fence itself was built on slightly raised ground and it's not that wet right next to it. We weren't talking about a little bit of water. We were talking about a directed torrent of saltwater aimed straight at it.

We, me and Raf that is, left at midday. There was a settlement we could make out on a hill to the north-east and we reckoned we could make it there by sunset if we really went for it. They should let us stay the night – that's the normal etiquette with traders anyway – but we made sure we had mosquito repellent, nets and plenty of dried food and water in case we were turned away and had to kip out in the open. There was obviously no guarantee that they'd have spades but most settlements seemed pretty well equipped and as there were no houses left standing anywhere near us it was not like we had a million other options.

Lee shot us an instruction as we left.

'No extras.'

My confusion must have shown on my face.

'Don't tell anyone what we're doing or they'll want to

come with us. We can't take anyone else. The more of us there are, the greater the risk of being caught.'

I nodded my agreement. It was harsh and my heart rebelled against it. Against depriving others of a chance to leave this malarial graveyard. But this wasn't about rescuing a few souls anymore. There was more at stake here. This was about bringing down an entire system.

Walking was slower going than I'd expected, probably because me and Raf were loaded up like beasts of burden. On top of our usual backpacks, over our shoulders balanced a thick stick from which hung ten skinned rabbits on one side and twenty reed torches on the other. We were like freaky deformed versions of the scales of justice statue outside the Justice Building back home. Home. The word sounds weird now. Foreign, somehow.

Anyway, walking was hard going and, to make things worse, our initial attempts at conversation all went horribly wrong too. I'd asked Raf how he was feeling, whether his head hurt, whether his vision was pixilating and instead of answering properly he just snapped back that I had to stop asking that and start trusting that he was OK. Which seemed terribly unfair as I was only being concerned, rationally concerned I might add, given the circumstances and his regular headaches. Then he commented that Jack seemed really well now and there was something about the way he stressed the word really, so that it came out as *R-E-A-L-L-Y*, that got my back up and we ended up having this malc argument that went a bit like this:

Me: 'Don't do that. We've resolved everything. Jack's not an issue.'

Raf: 'I don't know what you're talking about.'

Me: 'So why the *R-E-A-L-L-Y* then?

Raf: 'You're being paranoid.'

Me: 'I'm *R-E-A-L-L-Y* not.'

There was about an hour of uncomfortable silent marching after this as we both focused inwards. Turns out carrying a massively heavy load is even harder if your muscles are an extra bit clenched from anger.

It was all beginning to get a bit too much for me, so I stopped and started doing something really mature like repeatedly kicking a molehill.

'Noa.' Raf's voice just behind me. Slow. Quiet. 'I'm sorry, OK? I'm really sorry. The headaches freak me out too. But I shouldn't have taken it out on you. I know that. And, as for the whole Jack thing, you're right, I probably was trying to make a point. Maybe subconsciously even. I'm an idiot. It's just he's all recovered now. And so tall. And so strong! And good with children. I mean, if I was a girl I might…'

And then he did this little pretend shiver of excitement, accompanied by his toothiest lopsided grin and all my anger melted away.

'Denser,' I laughed, turning my back to him. 'Absolute, total denser.'

In response I felt a tap on my shoulder and span round to see the front leg of a stripped rabbit moving along to a whispered voiceover from my loser boyfriend.

'I am the ghost of the dead bunny come to haunt you. Run little rabbit, run.'

I shot about a metre up in the air – a dead skinned rabbit's face is particularly horrific close up – and then kicked him in the shin.

'That makes no sense at all!' I shot back. 'Why would a rabbit even say that?' dissolving into laughter despite myself.

'You're very sexy when you laugh, Noa Blake. We should never fight. Never again – deal?'

And then he stuck out the dead rabbit's paw again for me to shake and I swivelled away just in time and set off running across the marshland, Raf's intentionally malc, ghostly 'whoo whoo hoo' chasing at my heels.

We reached the settlement just as the sun was starting to bleed into the evening sky. I was worried that it was going to be like the first one we'd come across in the Wetlands, the one that had refused us entry, the one that didn't trade anymore. But when we knocked at the outer fence and called out our presence we were met with an open door and two pairs of friendly eyes, eyes which lit up at the sight of fresh rabbit.

We were taken to their leader, a less friendly, wiry man with flint grey eyes and a totally bald head, who smelt the rabbits (to confirm if they were fresh, not because he was a complete weirdo) and then readily negotiated an exchange. Four spades and a night's accommodation for the rabbits and torches. He produced the spades for us to inspect from a corrugated iron lean-to near the entrance and then replaced them to 'keep them safe till morning'. Safe from what exactly, I don't know. Maybe just so we didn't try and do a runner with the spades and the rabbits.

Luckily enough for us, animals seem to be scarce in this area. The land must be really low lying as, even though it wasn't that close to the sea, it was pretty flooded. This was the first fresh meat they'd had for weeks. The thin but happy, visibly salivating faces round the communal fire later were testament to this. Spades and general equipment on the other hand were plentiful as the settlement was near this old, half-submerged town, which they'd fully stripped.

Talk waited until plates had been licked clean and all that was left was a pile of small white bones. Then we felt all eyes swivel in our direction, curious, expectant. It took a few seconds before I realised what they wanted from us. Then it clicked. We were supposed to be traders. Traders brought news. Clarity must have hit Raf at the same time.

'So…' he began. 'We bring news.'

I get it – neither of us could remember how traders began their news sharing spiel. It felt right that it should have some formality or ritual to it. But this! Raf sounded like he was reciting lines from a terrible play. He might as well have gone all the way with an *oh yay oh yay, we here be town criers.* There were a couple of badly covered-up sniggers and Raf flushed red but forced himself to continue.

'The Raiders have been defeated.'

Sniggers were forgotten and in their place rose up a loud hum of indistinct chatter that rippled outwards like water in a disturbed pond.

'So it's true then,' a voice came from the other end of the table. A guy in his thirties, or maybe younger. People age pretty badly out here.

'A trader came by a couple of days ago. Said he'd come across their settlement burnt to the ground, but we weren't sure we could trust him seeing as no one knew where their settlement was. How can we trust you?'

Raf hesitated but I could see the need in their eyes and understood it. The need to know that you're safe. That your children are safe.

'We were there,' I said. Raf kicked me sharply under the table and I bit back a yelp.

'But,' a woman's voice this time. I sought her out. She was young with a couple of wriggling toddlers in her lap. Worry lines creased her gaunt face. 'But you're traders?'

'There was a group of us,' I clarified. 'A battle. The Raiders are gone though, I promise. That's all that matters.'

Raf was shooting daggers at me, but what did he want me to do? I couldn't take back what I'd already said. And these people deserved to know.

'Which direction did you come from today?' The leader's voice was raised but tightly controlled. Cold. His eyes narrowed to flecks of steel.

I opened my mouth, but Raf answered first.

'The east.'

A lie.

'No they didn't,' piped a child's voice from behind. *From the mouth of babes.* 'I was playing with Sam and we saw them come in from the west, over Ridges Marsh.'

The leader's face darkened. He ran a hand over his smooth head as if massaging his thoughts into alignment.

'You're breaking out, aren't you?' It was an accusation rather than a question.

Sixtyish pairs of eyes now bore into us. I could feel the heat of them, probing for the truth.

'No.' Raf's voice was hard.

What had I done? Denser. Denser. Denser.

'No,' I echoed firmly, trying to undo the damage.

The leader put his head on one side and tapped his upturned ear aggressively, as if trying to shake out the lies.

'You expect us to believe that a group of you, a group

that is big enough to defeat the Raiders, a group that's based to the west, where the Fence is, just happens to want spades?'

'Take us with you!'

'Take me!'

'Take us all!'

The air was ripped with plaintive cries. I stared at the ground, wishing that a spade was in my hand now so that I could tunnel my way out of there. But I couldn't. We were here. Trapped.

The air felt static from tension, that heavy sparky quality you get just before a thunderstorm. Raf stood.

'Give us the night to decide.' It came out as more of a command than a request and the confidence with which he spoke must have given him a measure of authority as people made space for us to get down from the table and retreat to our shack. We were conscious of being followed every step of the way.

'I'm so sorry, Raf,' I whispered as soon as we were inside.

'There's no time to think about that, now. We need to focus on what we do next.'

Raf's face was a mask of concentration. I know I had no right to expect forgiveness, comfort, but I felt cut up inside and a few kind words would have helped stop the guilt haemorrhaging out of me.

'We can't tell them. We can't take them with us,' I said, stating the obvious.

'I know.'

'So?'

'We leave when everyone's asleep.'

'What if they're guarding us?'

'We use what Megan taught us,' came the grim reply.

But we couldn't, could we? Couldn't kill good people. Innocent people. What was it that Annie had said back at the Peak, the first settlement that had really welcomed me and Raf in the Wetlands – never lose your humanity. Was anything worth that?

The hours dragged by in slow motion as we waited for total darkness to fall. For the noise and chatter of the settlement to still. And then waited some more just to be certain. My ears felt like they were vibrating, tingling, they were so alert to our surroundings. The tiniest creak magnified a hundredfold.

Raf called it.

'It's time.'

I went first. Maybe to prove something, to compensate, I don't know. Tentatively I pushed the rusty door. It opened a couple of centimetres with a squeak that sounded like a fanfare. A bugle announcing our presence.

'Hello?' A voice. Male. Our sort of age.

I was right. They'd put a guard on our door. Sometimes being right sucks.

I fought down the panic that was spreading through my body, liquefying bones. I wanted to sob, to ask Raf to fix it, but I knew this was my fault. My problem. I had to silence him. The boy. No, *the guard*. That was how to do it. Objectify the enemy. See them as a thing, an 'it' not a 'him'. The mantra, Megan's mantra for silent killing started playing in my brain – a tune on repeat. Wait until the target was three metres away then: arm, wrap, neck, squeeze.

Arm

wrap

neck

squeeze.

'Please could you come in a moment?' I didn't recognise my own voice. Didn't want to.

The door creaked open further and a red-haired boy appeared in the doorframe, semi-silhouetted in the light of his reed torch. His eyes were wide, his smile genuine. He reminded me of Jack and the resemblance was a kick to the kidneys.

'Sorry to be guarding you and everything,' he said with an apologetic grin.

Stop being so nice. Stop being so nice.

He started to enter and I was watching the distance. 4m, 3.5m…

My legs were propelling me forward. My arms ready to grab, twist and spin.

'NO!' Raf grabbed my elbow just in time.

'Stop Noa,' he hissed. 'You're right. We can't do this. This is wrong. Some things are just too wrong.'

The boy's face was a collage of confusion and fear.

'What's going on?'

The next word out of his mouth was going to be help. A loud, yelled help. I knew it. I acted instinctively.

'Put your hand over his mouth,' I hissed at Raf. This could work for a few seconds at most but we needed a longer-term solution, a proper gag. The boy was already wriggling out of Raf's grip. There was no time to reach my pack. Without thinking I whipped off my t-shirt and then removed Raf's hand for the split second needed to stuff it into the boy's mouth.

It stopped the scream. Instead it was nearly Raf that gave us away. This loud snort laugh erupted out of his mouth. I guess I looked pretty ridiculous standing there in my grey bra, stuffing a t-shirt into the mouth of a strange boy like some special type of pervert.

Raf managed to pull himself together enough to tie the boy up and secure the gag, using the rope we'd used to hang the rabbits and torches.

Then we flung our backpacks on and were off. Zigzagging down the paths that ran between the shacks. Left. Right. Left. Left. Right. We were back at the main entrance. Raf was about to push open the gate when I yanked him back.

'We're forgetting something. Spades.'

We raced the few metres to the lean-to and Raf pulled out six spades.

'I know we agreed four,' he said between pants of breath, 'but now we'll each have one. And I figure the deal's kind of broken anyway!'

Something caught my attention at the back of the lean-to and I reached in behind Raf, pulling out two pairs of hedging shears ('For cutting,' I hissed at Raf's surprised face. '*Wire* cutting') and a couple of reed torches as well and we then were off for real, racing down the hill and into the shallows, water obscuring footprints.

We stumbled into camp before sunrise. We were both wet, bedraggled and exhausted. We'd probably walked the longest, wettest route possible, having only dared light the reed torches when we had put the settlement far behind us, meaning that we'd splashed through or fallen into mile upon mile of swampy marshland first. I kept thinking I heard noises behind us – footsteps, the occasional twig snapping – but Raf said I was being paranoid, that the stress had fried my nerves. I was so grateful to see the familiar layout of sleeping bags and mosquito nets that a massive smile spread across my face. Well, spread until it was wiped out by a hard karate chop to the neck and I hit the floor.

'Wh—at?' My voice came out all weird and squeaky from my very probably permanently damaged windpipe. My assailant straddled me and hissed a dire, blood-curdling warning about what she'd do to me if I made another noise.

I knew that voice.

'Ella?'

Ella apologetically climbed off me, and I instantly forgave her, obviously. She'd been on guard duty. On look out in case anyone from the Ministry came back.

'Remind me never to cross you for real,' I squeak-laughed through sore, crushed ribs.

Our scuffle had woken the rest of the camp.

'Why are you back so early?' came Lee's sleep-infused voice as he lit a reed torch so we could see each other properly. 'Didn't they have any spades?'

'No, we've got them. Six in fact,' Raf was quick to answer. 'There was some hostility, though, so we thought it was best to get out of there.'

I reached towards Raf and squeezed his arm to say thanks. Thanks for not ratting me out as the loser who nearly ruined the whole mission.

There might have been more questions if it hadn't been for Lee's next comment.

'Noa, why are you just wearing a bra?'

'Long story,' I replied. 'I'm kind of down a t-shirt.'

'Take mine. Cover yourself up,' from Jack, anger seeping into his voice. Like I'd flung off my shirt in wild abandon during some big love-in session with Raf rather than used it to gag a guard. I didn't like being judged. Not by anyone. Especially not by someone who was supposed to be my friend, so I clammed up. He didn't deserve an explanation. He could think what he liked. And keep his t-shirt.

Lee went to fetch me his spare one. He'd been using it to wrap round the satellite part but figured that a millimetre of cotton probably wasn't offering that much protection and, in all probability, the circuitry was damaged beyond repair anyway.

'It's probably best we waste no time though. Start digging at first light,' Raf advised when Lee returned. 'The guys at the settlement really weren't happy and there's a chance they'll come looking for us.'

Digging began at dawn. My body craved rest but my brain barked orders at it to continue. Told it that it could shut down later. The original plan had been to dig at night, to reduce the chances of being spotted by any Ministry plane or helicopter that might randomly fly over, but now time was the main factor – the risk of the other settlement sabotaging our plans was the most immediate danger.

Lee and Ella had marked out the best point of attack. The river wasn't the closest to the Fence at this point but it was straight which meant that it was flowing the fastest and therefore had the most power. Next to this spot, Jack had already begun to stockpile logs and rocks, some almost boulder sized. How the hell had he managed to lift them? His strength was staggering. We stood there for a minute. Clutching our spades and staring at the Fence. An abstract plan suddenly becoming real. Horribly real. And it was my plan. The responsibility was a crushing weight.

There was no obvious place to cross the river, no conveniently placed stepping stones, or fallen log, so we all had to wade across, water up to our waists, bags and equipment held aloft by upstretched arms. On the other side, Lee assumed control by drawing a line in the earth a few metres from the bank. He cleared his throat.

'Right. So first we dig the new channel from here directly to…' he waved the spade in the direction of the Fence rather than saying the word. 'We only breach the wall of the existing channel as the final step.'

The rest of us were still glued to the edge of the riverbank, digging heels into stones and looping toes under riverweed. Hoping to be caught and tethered in its tendrils. It felt like the Fence was looking at us. Could sense our plan. No one wanted to go first. To be the first to slice their spade into the ground.

Finally, Jack took a step forward and drove his spade into the earth. There was a collective intake of breath and stilling of hearts. We waited. Waited for an alarm to sound. For soldiers to pounce. For machine guns to fire.

But there was nothing.

Just the sound of a spade slicing wet earth and the thud of the mud landing to the side.

I've always been good at facial recognition. Weirdly so. There used to be this advert on the telly, flashing up image after image in rapid succession – faces front on/in profile/in shadow – just glimpses really, and you were supposed to try and see if any matched. At the end some wording was stamped across the screen. *Think you have what it takes to be part of our elite identification team? Call this number…* I would jump around the lounge shouting, 'Me, me, they should pick me; I'm really good at this!' and I remember not understanding why my parents weren't prouder and more encouraging. I get it now. Get what the team actually does. Whose faces they are trying to spot.

We'd been digging for nearly a whole day and I'd reached breaking point. Marching all night instead of sleeping does that to you. Raf had fallen over moments before and had to lie down with his eyes shut as he was assaulted by another of his headaches.

'It's nothing,' he'd claimed, pushing me away, hating his weakness. But his eyes were cloudy from pain and his voice was angry, cold, distant – not like normal Raf at all. 'Give me some space, Noa. A little space occasionally would be nice.'

So maybe it was just the fatigue and the added stress of Raf's sudden personality change, but I'm certain I saw the face of the boy from the settlement peering out from behind a cluster of trees in the distance. The boy guard. It was a long way but I was sure I was right. My heart starting beating out of sync. A jazz rhythm. They'd found us. They were going to sabotage our mission.

'Describe him,' Ella demanded.

'He had red hair, and … normal build. Everything else was normal, OK … I can't explain but it was him, I know it was.'

Being able to spot isn't the same as being able to explain.

The creases between Ella's eyebrows deepened.

'You probably just saw Jack,' Ella said gently, in that voice that's reserved for frail people who've been hit on the head one too many time.

'No. No. There was someone. They've found us,' I insisted.

Lee went off to look but came back having found nothing, not bothering to disguise his annoyance at having wasted precious digging time.

'Noa, you need to sleep.'

'No...'

'For everyone's sake. There's no reason to believe anyone's following us. No reason to believe they know what we're doing.'

I opened my mouth. I should have confessed everything. Should have told the rest of them how I'd messed up and that the settlement knew we were trying to break out but I didn't. I kept quiet like the coward that I am.

In the end I obeyed them. They didn't give me a choice. And I started to lose faith. Maybe it wasn't the boy from the camp. Maybe there hadn't even been a boy at all and my mind was just starting to hallucinate from exhaustion. I went back to camp and closed my eyes and sleep instantly overtook me. I'm not sure how long I slept for but the new channel was considerably longer by the time I woke and rejoined the group. Raf was back too, spade in hand. I sought his eyes but he avoided mine.

Everyone was digging and the air rang with the slice-thud of earth being cut away and discarded. Now over a metre deep and two metres wide, the channel ran perpendicularly from just behind the river bank to within spitting distance of the Fence itself. Hollowed out, with its walls of freshly turned earth it resembled a mass grave.

After a few more hours' work in the fading light, Lee finally put down his spade. 'That's enough for today, everyone,' he declared, exhausted but satisfied with our progress. 'Tomorrow we breach the bank.'

What he didn't say but what everyone said in their heads was *Tomorrow, tomorrow we cross the Fence.*

I used to think the man in the moon was happy. Back in the days when a magical Santa and tooth fairy were my accepted truths, it totally made sense to me that the man in the moon might be a living thing too. A body-less, benevolent sphere-head, floating around, giving us tides and playing slow motion peek-a-boo. Me and Daisy would stare out of our windows on sleepovers when there was a full moon and look up at his smiling face. Daisy even made up a rhyme: *Moon head, moon head, give us sweet dreams in our bed.* She started off with moon face, but face is harder to rhyme.

Now though, lying on the hard ground and unable to sleep, the moon's mouth doesn't seem to be smiling at all. It seems to be open in an unending scream.

At breakfast I found that I wasn't the only one who hadn't slept much last night. There were no cobwebs of sleep to dust off. Everyone seemed wired, ready. Cortisol maxed. Backpacks were loaded. Spades picked up. Hedge cutters sharpened with stones.

Jack dug the final section of the new channel. This took him very nearly to the Fence itself and every muscle in my body was clenched until the last thud of earth fell and he stepped away whole. Not a burnt charcoal statue. Not shredded by bullets. But alive.

Now came the hardest part. We had to dam the existing river and then, just as it was about to flood, break the right-hand bank to force the water into the new channel, towards the Fence. We needed to build an underwater wall strong enough to hold back the force of the river. Our initial attempts at hurling in stones and sticks weren't the greatest success. Many simply rolled away or were carried off by the current. Then Jack had a brainwave. Lying not far from the left bank of the river was the stump of a charred skeletal tree, roots torn from the ground and exposed, a lightning strike casualty. Like soldiers carrying a battering ram, Jack had us pick up and march the trunk back to the stream, dropping it in with a tidal wave of a splash. The trunk rolled over once, twice, then stopped as we let up a cheer and shook out aching arms. Jack was now in charge. Under his instruction we stood, half of us on each bank, hurled in the biggest rocks and logs we could find and watched as they collected in front of the log and started to stack, locking together with a chink and a clunk. Foundations we could build upon. I didn't manage to lift and throw anything bigger than about child-head size, but Jack, face red and arms shaking from strain, managed to launch in a proper boulder that soaked everyone in a shower of water. Raf snorted at this feat of Herculean strength – but it came out more snide than anything.

As the wall started to take shape and rise, me and Raf took up position on the floor of the newly dug channel, ready to break the bank when the time came. Nell was with us as she lacked the brute strength for throwing. Digging seemed easier.

We stood on the channel floor, spades poised, ready. Before long the river bank in front of us was beginning to bulge from the pressure of the trapped water that sent fine cracks of strain running across its breadth like lines in glazed pottery.

Splash. Crash. Jack, Lee and Ella continued to hurl in rocks.

The cracks were multiplying and widening.

I could feel sweat start to trickle down my forehead.

'Get ready!'

We raised our shovels, aiming them at the river bank. I could feel my breath flow past my lips. In … out … in … out.

'NOW!'

As Lee shouted the signal, everything became a bit of a blur.

With a jabbing motion I started to attack the wall of the bank, eating into it with short, sharp thrusts.

A shower of water hit me as Jack threw a massive stone into the river. There were more splashes, creaks and grunts from effort. The earth in the wall was thinning, becoming wetter with each onslaught until it was sliding off the spade, each hole rapidly filling with water. More attacks from our spades and the wall started to bulge properly, moving towards me like a face emerging from the mud. I'm not sure of the order of what came next, it all happened so fast. The wall of the bank becoming thinner and thinner and sagging towards us. Lee's voice shouting at us to hurry up. And then Raf's spade cutting all the way through.

We'd planned to break the bank apart slowly. Make three or four holes and then enlarge them.

It didn't happen like that.

The pressure from the dammed water was much stronger than we'd anticipated and the pierced bank fell away as one like a piece of shattered glass, the water rushing to meet us. Me and Raf were stood in the centre of the new channel. Nell was meant to be at the edge. She wasn't meant to be anywhere near the middle.

'Out! Get out!' Raf shouted as he clambered up and out of the channel. He reached for my hand and I turned to take it when I saw the water hit Nell. It knocked her off her feet, so she was sprawled on the floor, the water pouring over her face. Over eyes, blocking nostrils, into her mouth. And then towards the Fence. She was spluttering, choking but that wasn't the real danger. As soon as the water hit the Fence, for a split second before the circuit went down, the water would be live. Electrified. Nell would be fried. I ran towards her, the resistance of the water slowing my stride into a slow-motion run.

'Noa, come back!' Raf yelled. 'There's no time! You'll both die. Come back!'

My hand grabbed Nell's wrist and I pulled her towards me, towards the edge, my whole body straining from the effort. I couldn't stop. I couldn't give up. I blocked Nell's screams as I yanked her arm too hard. Blocked Raf's repeated yells to save myself. Blocked Ella's yells of panic as she saw what was going on. Blocked it all. Suddenly there was a splash beside me and Raf was there too. Holding Nell's other arm. Together we pulled her the final metre to the bank and threw ourselves out the water.

A second later a wall of water hit the Fence. There was a huge yellow spark. A blinding flash and the water bubbled. Dead fish after dead fish floated upwards, silvering the surface.

We'd done it. We'd achieved the impossible. We'd turned the Fence off. But no one felt like celebrating. Ella ran at Raf, claws drawn, and seeking blood.

'How could you! You'd have let her fry! You frickin' freakoid!'

She spat at him and it took all of Jack's strength to hold her back, but he needn't have bothered. A fight was the least of our problems.

Nee-Nah-Nee-Nah.

The air around us was being torn apart and our eardrums felt like they were about to explode. The Fence short-circuiting had triggered a smaller emergency circuit. A siren. Wailing out news of our attack.

We knew that somewhere in a Ministry building a red light would be flashing. A sister siren screaming. Within minutes they'd be launching a helicopter. Coming to investigate. Coming to get us.

We looked to Lee. He wasn't saying anything.

'Come on. We need to go. Now!' Raf took control. 'Who's got the cutters?'

I picked up a pair and Jack retrieved the other from his backpack.

We sprinted to the Fence. Our fear of discovery had stripped it of its power somehow. Tiptoeing, creeping was no longer an option. Fear was a luxury we didn't have time for.

'How do we know the Fence is definitely down?' Nell asked quietly, stammering over the first couple of words.

'We don't,' came Jack's grim answer as he opened the jaws of the hedge trimmer wide and locked them around a wire joint at the bottom of the Fence. I felt the bile hit the back of my throat and I closed my eyes. Opening them again, Jack was still there. Still standing. I started laughing. Manically, like a crazy person, until Ella gave my arm a savage pinch and told me to get a grip.

Jack was putting all his strength behind the cutters. His biceps shook and his face flamed redder and redder as he tried to force the handles together. To cut.

'I ... I can't. The wire's too thick.'

We stared through the criss-cross wires. Animals in a trap. With the hunter on his way.

'What now?' Nell's voice. Small, scared.

We looked around desperately. Left, right, forward, back.

Up.

At the top of the Fence, ten metres or so above our heads rose the mosquito grids. The pattern of wire changed. They were made of thinner netting.

'We climb,' I said emotionlessly.

On my instruction we removed shoes and socks and stuffed them into backpacks along with the cutters. Then, hooking fingers and toes into wire diamonds, we began to scale the Fence. The wire cut into our hands and feet, claiming skin, and my arms began to shake from the strain and crazy levels of adrenalin. I've never been good with heights. Even walking down a particularly steep hill can give me mini palpitations. This was something else. *Don't look down*, I kept repeating. My new mantra. *Don't look down. Focus ahead. Pick a diamond. Edge up. Pick another diamond.* Someone, Daisy I think, once told me that in lots of action films where someone looks like they're hanging off a vertical drop, they're just filming with the camera on its side, so the actor's actually lying down on the floor. I tried to convince my brain that this was happening here. *You're just crawling along the floor on a big wire mesh. Nothing can go wrong. This is all pretend.* There was a scream to my right. Ella had lost her toe hold and was suspended by her arms. They looked unnaturally long, the weight of her body practically dislocating them from their sockets.

'Help! Help! Oh God, help!'

I looked down and my head swam. We were at least six metres in the air. Forget about the Ministry, if Ella fell she'd die or at least be paralysed. Death but just slower.

'You can do this, Ella,' I had to shout to be heard over the siren and the volume seemed to force confidence into my voice. Replaced the tremor with reassurance.

'Lift your right foot up.'

'I can't!'

'You can. Just a couple of centimetres. Perfect. Now hook your big toe round the join. Yes. Left a fraction. There!'

Ella hooked her foot into position and her arms stopped shaking. I burst into tears and then had to force myself to deep breathe so that I didn't black out.

Four metres to go and we'd be at the grids. Four. Three. Two.

We were there. Jack had one pair of cutters, I had the other. Raf and Ella spidered over so that they could stand just behind us, their bodies locking us into position while we twisted round to untie the cutters from our packs. Fingers fumbling, we removed the safety catch to unlock the blades so that they opened into a big steel V. I picked a joint, a crossroad of wires and squeezed. It took three attempts. Three bites of the blade and then a hole. I gingerly moved the wire aside and pushed one of my hands through. For the first time in over two months, a part of me, about a twentieth of me, was back in the Territory.

I let out a cry, a victory whoop, which was quickly echoed by Jack as he too reached through.

We didn't get to celebrate for long. Our triumphant cries were drowned out by other sounds. Shouts. Noises we would have heard long ago if it hadn't been for the siren's continuing wail. Noises coming from behind us, like a battle cry. We tightened our grip on the wire and swivelled round to see them coming towards us. Running. Sixty-odd pairs of feet. The other settlement. All of them. I was right. They had been following us. They knew that this was their chance to break through the Fence too and they were determined to take it.

Raf barked instructions.

'Come on guys, move!'

It wasn't needed. Me and Jack were already widening the holes, cutting again and again until there were two openings, each the size of a small window.

'Faster!' Raf urged. 'This is taking too long.'

There was no time to think. I was next to one of the holes. I had to be first through it. Locking the toes of my left foot round a joint in the wire, I unhooked my right foot and pushed it through the opening followed by my bent over body. Severed wires scratched at my back and my knees started trembling. Shaking convulsively, threatening not to bear weight. *Come on*, I yelled internally. My right foot extended down the other side of the Fence, scrabbling for a hold. Finally my toes hooked on. I swung my left leg through too and I was there, fully in the Territory. Raf was right behind me. There was a cry to my left as Nell's backpack got caught on the wire and Jack, rather than try and gently unhook it, simply sliced the trapped fabric off. Nell was about to object but Jack silenced her with a single glance.

Seconds later Ella and Lee were through, too, and we were all on the other side, the Territory side, and beginning our descent. Going down was even harder than going up. Every move had to be made by feel, searching with fingers and then dropping down, hoping your feet would find a hold. Not only that but we were now facing the people from the settlement, who were about to start climbing. We were separated only by the interlocking wire. Animals and spectators at the zoo, unsure which was which.

Three quarters of the way down another sound overtook the siren and caught our ears. Caught our ears and froze our limbs.

Thuck-whop. Thuck-whop.

The blades of a Ministry helicopter cresting the horizon and bearing straight at us. It was black. And big. Much bigger than the last one. Curved like a scythe with two sets of blades. They were sending in the troops.

'Go, go, go!' I shouted.

We scrabbled down the last few metres, slipping and sliding. Lee lost his grip and tumbled to the ground and there were a horrific few seconds before he pulled himself up to standing and tested his legs, teetering forwards and backwards, a geriatric who'd lost his Zimmer frame. He straightened up and balanced. Weight evenly distributed. Nothing broken.

The people from the other settlement were now

swarming the Fence. They'd come so far. They weren't going to turn back now.

There was something about their bravery, their refusal to give up, that was magnetic. It caught your eyes and pulled.

'Come on, hide!' yelled Ella, grabbing my arm. We fell into crouch mode and ran for it, scuttling across the twenty or so metres of marram grass and then ducking into the Solar Fields as the helicopter came closer and closer. We were only about five rows in when we had to stop. Lee frantically signalling at us to get down. We flattened ourselves in a line behind and below the silver panels.

Had they seen us? It was impossible to tell. My breathing was keeping time with the helicopter blades; and the ground, the ground was shaking and dust was spiralling, dancing into our eyes and down our throats. The helicopter must have been directly overhead. It didn't land immediately. Didn't have to.

It was like a horror-show symphony. The staccato of gunfire punctuated by cries of pain, real bloodcurdling screams, and all the time the background siren continuing to wail. Lamenting the dead. I wanted to bury my fingers into my ears but I couldn't. I had caused this with my big mouth. I was responsible. The least I could do was listen.

The helicopter only landed once the firing had stopped.

'What's going on?' I whispered.

No one replied. No one knew.

'We need someone to go and see,' I repeated. 'We need to know if they're coming for us.'

No one volunteered until Ella volunteered Raf. She clearly hadn't forgiven him for the whole 'leave Nell to die' thing, totally overlooking the fact that if he hadn't gone back into the channel both she and I would be toast. One look at Raf's face told me he wasn't up for it. His skin had that greyish tinge again and his eyes weren't totally there.

'I'll go,' I said, with a gulp, as if fear was something edible that could be swallowed and digested.

The solar panels were arranged in long parallel rows. Fifteen or so attached to each other, then a small gap, then another fifteen and so on. I crept to the end of a row and peered out. Glimpse, retreat, glimpse. A nervous tortoise not sure whether to emerge from its shell. I saw the helicopter had touched down on the barren land right next to the Fence; then, as I watched, twenty pairs of boots jumped down. The siren stopped and the sudden quiet was almost unbearable. Normal noises: breathing, heartbeats, the scrape of toes across sand all suddenly audible. Magnified. It felt like a curtain had been whipped away and our position revealed with a cymbal crash. The commander, a guy with a messed-up nose and grey hair, was in the middle of the soldiers, shouting orders. There were ten or fifteen dead bodies strewn across the foot of the Fence on our side, the rest on the other. The ones in the Wetlands were left there, too much hassle to collect, or maybe as a message – a modern equivalent of heads on spikes; the ones on our side were thrown into the helicopter. There was nothing to do but watch as the bodies were being dragged along the ground by their feet, face down. I flinched as they bounced over pebbles or scraped against rocks and shuddered as it hit me that they couldn't feel pain. Their faces could bash against a hundred rocks and it wouldn't matter. Nothing would matter to them again as they were dead. All dead.

One soldier looked younger than the rest. He had blond hair, cropped tight to his skull highlighting ears that projected at right angles from his face. I'd noticed him because he seemed to avert his eyes when carrying the bodies, which he'd slung over his shoulder rather than dragged along the ground.

The soldiers had walkie-talkies but they weren't using them. They were shouting to each other instead.

'Any walkers?'

'Best do a sweep to be sure.'

No! I yelled in my head. *Don't sweep. Go home. Go back.*

They fanned out and I stopped breathing and closed my eyes.

We'd be okay unless they came straight at us. The marram grass meant there were no footprints, no breadcrumb trail to follow.

I forced my eyes open again.

No one was going in the direction of Raf and the others so if they stayed still they'd be fine, but the young blond soldier was walking towards me. Straight at me.

There used to be this guy in the same block as us in the Territory who claimed he could bend spoons with his mind: focus all his energy on them and then kind of wilt them over. He said he'd been trained as a weapon by the army. He was a total nutter but right now I decided to believe. I'd bend the soldier's path. Channelling every cell of my being, I willed him to divert. *Go left.* No, that might take him towards the others. *Go right. Turn your feet right.* But he didn't. He came down the row. Slowly, steadily. Straight at me. I couldn't run. That'd be worse. It's the movement of prey that draws the predators. That's why rabbits freeze. Sometimes it's your best bet.

He was so close I could hear his breathing.

All it would take was for him to bend over the panel and I'd be exposed.

He looked forward, off into the distance.

Then he bent down.

There was this retching sound. Over and over. His stomach contents emptied fifty centimetres to my right. He looked up. This was it. I thought I'd scream but I didn't. This terrible sense of calm came over me. I was there but I wasn't. The world didn't really exist. Our eyes met. Locked. His were blue. Blue with yellow flecks. Mum used to have a dress like that. Buttercups against a summer sky. I'd tell him it was just me. I was the only one who'd made it. The others still had a chance.

'Report in,' came the yell from the grey-haired boss guy.

'Negative.'

'Negative.'

'Negative.'

Reports were shouted back and I gave up a prayer of thanks that the others hadn't been found. It was just me.

The boy soldier stood up. My head swirled. I couldn't feel my toes anymore.

'Negative.'

He walked away without glancing back and once he was back in the helicopter I started retching myself.

Life's messed up. Evil and good swimming round each other, often wearing each other's clothes.

The Solar Fields give me the creeps. Like a kind of alien futurescape. Row upon row of head-height, shining silver shields, sat at 45 degrees to the earth. Rising over hills, dipping into valleys. Harnessing and storing the sun's energy. We were used to panels on top of buildings, obviously. Every south- or west-facing building in the First City had one. Had to by law. That glint that always caught the corner of your eye. But nothing like this. This was a regiment. An army. You had to shade your eyes and squint just to look at them. And the most alienating thing of all was there was nothing else. No trees, they'd all been cleared. No long grass. No animals. Just metal, panels and light. The only natural thing I could make out was a stream winding its way through the middle, coming from the higher ground to the west. A silver snake reflecting the panels above.

The soldiers returned at dusk. We were already a few miles from the Fence, the aim at this point just being to get away, when we heard the blades once more. We hit the earth and lay there as the helicopters, two of them, approached.

Nell lay shivering next to me, fear mirroring hypothermia.

'They've come back for us, haven't they?'

I didn't know what to say. All it would have taken was for the blond soldier, my soldier as I thought of him, to have broken down later during some sort of debrief. To have had a pang of guilt. To have told the others or his boss about me. They would be back. With reinforcements.

'Noa?' Nell again, but I couldn't bring myself to answer her. Raf broke into the silence.

'No. No, I don't think they have.'

If it had been lighter and my face hadn't been buried into the ground, Raf would have seen my raised eyebrow.

'The helicopters are a different colour – dark green not black.'

Somewhere to my left, Jack snorted.

'There's more,' Raf continued, a metallic note to his voice, raised now as the thuck-whop was getting louder and louder. 'These have got lights on, obviously, as it's getting dark, but not full-on search beams. They're not looking for us. They're not looking for anyone.'

'Then why are they here?' Ella this time.

'To mend the hole!' Lee said, with an audible exclamation mark. 'Of course. They couldn't leave the Fence down with the mosquito grids shredded. They're not soldiers, they're builders – engineers.'

Still, we weren't taking any chances. We went without dinner and curled up in a line under the panels. No one could sleep, not with the enemy so close, so instead we played stupid games until the helicopters left again. Ella suggested Never Have I Ever which should have been ridiculous as the strongest thing we had to drink was stream water and there were so many topics that were a total no-go area. Still, somehow we played it. Instead of drinking you had to click your fingers if it applied to you. Turns out Jack can't click his fingers, which was hilarious in itself. You'd just hear this weird scrape-thud sound through the dark. And instead of trying to catch people out, instead of trying to find out their dirty secrets, it turned into a weird kind of group bonding thing.

Never have I ever taken part in a battle against psycho Raiders. Click, click, click, click, click, scrape-thud.

Never have I ever scaled an electric fence. Click, click, click, click, click, scrape-thud.

And so on.

The hours passed and we weren't afraid.

We probably got no more than two hours sleep as the helicopters only left fractionally before dawn. Breakfast was a hastily devoured couple of dried rabbit strips that seemed to leave us hungrier than we started, but hunger's kind of become our default setting so the cramps and rumbles are getting easier and easier to ignore. Once we were 'fed' and packed, all eyes turned to Ella.

She was in charge now. Well, of directions anyway. It was Ella who'd seen the Server, the place where they stored and transmitted the uploads, even though she hadn't known what it was at the time.

We followed behind, walking when she walked and pausing when she paused, hoping to God she'd get us there. There was no plan B. It's not like she had the Server's GPS coordinates or anything, but there were things she knew. Stuff we could work with. The Fence had been visible but not close. Sat on the horizon like a play fence from a toy farm. So, step one, we headed inland until the Fence receded to the right sort of size. Ella and Aunty

Vicki had been heading north towards the Arable Lands. It was on the third day of non-stop marching through the Solar Fields that they'd been caught, so it meant chances were that we were currently south of our destination. Step two, we marched north. Ella also said the Server hadn't been the only building they'd passed. There were others, of a similar size, squat brick structures, where they probably stored spare parts or where the workers who kept the Solar Fields functioning were based. Something like that anyway. The difference about the Server, apart from the hum, which we'd probably only notice when we were reasonably close, was its tall, thin mast. Ella recalled it with a shudder. She said it was one of the reasons they'd stopped there. She'd been so exhausted she had to rest or she'd collapse and the mast with its high cross-like antenna had reminded her of a church, a spire, so she'd thought they'd be safe there. Protected. Her laugh had this brittle quality. A bark crossed with a swallowed sob.

A mast made sense. They'd have to have some way of sending the uploads back to the Cities. And its height would help. We should be able to spot it from a way off.

We set up camp before dusk, knowing we needed to find food while it was still light. We still had some dried meat and seaweed but supplies were getting low. Lower than anyone felt comfortable with. There was no open ground, no glade or circle of trees to shelter under. It was more a question of picking a row and putting our things down between some panels. I wanted to talk to Raf; I needed to. Last night, our malc game had distracted me, filled the void, but today I couldn't get the images of the dead bodies out of my brain. Couldn't block the sound of the machine guns mowing them down. My guilt was like superglue, clamping the pictures in position behind my eyelids, not to be dislodged. There was no getting away from them. Closing my eyes only heightened the colours, like a TV screen in the dark. Raf had wandered off, lying down a distance from the others. I followed him. His eyes were closed but I could tell that he wasn't actually asleep. Deep breath in. I started trying to talk, but immediately got my head bitten off.

'Not now, Noa. I need some space. You're always here. Always bothering me.'

Each word was like a blow dart. A poison-laced sting. Even his tone was different. Harsh, snappy. It was like he didn't only dislike me, but he actually hated me a bit. And like 'he' wasn't Raf anymore. Again. Like some bodysnatcher had stolen his skin and was hiding out there for a while. I couldn't handle this now. The stress was already too much for me and I felt like I was breaking, cracking. I needed support not abuse.

I bit my lip to stop myself from crying. Bit it hard until a metallic taste filled my mouth. If he was going to be a dick like this, I wasn't going to let him see me cry. No. No way. Not even if it meant every swallow I took was tinged with blood.

I stood up, unsteadily, and returned to the others, weaving, colliding twice with the sides of the panels on the way and bruising my hip in the process.

I scanned the group for a friendly face, a confidant. Ella was out with Lee collecting water, but she wouldn't have been my first choice anyway as she's not exactly a pom-pom waving Raf fangirl. I could just imagine her saying: *Well, what do you expect from a freakoid?*

Nell was sprawled out on the ground, her white skin and hair almost luminous amongst the silver. She looked otherworldly and, for once, at peace. It would have been cruel to disturb her and she was too young to have to deal with my boyfriend issues. To be honest, I was also a bit embarrassed that they would seem massively trivial to her. *Hey, girl who had her parents die, was rejected by her settlement and then kept as a slave for a year, I'm having a really tough time of it as my boyfriend was mean to me…*

That left … well, that left Jack.

Jack was leaving to forage for dinner and I ran to catch him up. He took one look at me and didn't say anything. Guess he knows me so well he didn't have to. He just looped his hand round my arm, gave me a bag to carry and told me not to scare the animals. We didn't find any animals. Unsurprisingly they kept their distance from the rows of silver panels. Maybe there was a noise, a hum too low or high for human hearing, that freaked them out. I remember, back when there were farmers and actual sheep, there being all this stuff about the hum from solar panels and wind turbines driving animals mad. Milk yields falling, people acting a bit crazy. Or maybe this time it was simpler. I looked at the bare earth with its odd patchy tufts of thick, dry grass. Maybe there just wasn't anything for animals to eat.

So what were we going to do? I was beginning to despair when we rounded the end of the row and took a right.

'Look!' Jack's voice low, excited.

There in front of us were clusters of yellow and brown mushrooms sprouting under a panel, forcing their way through the soil to the surface – some bulbous, some umbrella shaped, some small, some huge, veined and spotted. Food sprouting through the earth into our fingers. It almost seemed too easy.

'What do you think?' Jack asked, still whispering. 'Roast mushroom for dinner?'

'Sure. It's basically Mucor, right?' I replied. 'And we probably don't need to whisper. Mushrooms aren't like rabbits, you know, they don't run away.'

Jack flashed a grin and punched me in the arm. I laughed too and it was cathartic. A release. For a second things were easy. I could forget where I was, what I'd done, everything I'd seen. It was like I'd stumbled into a time machine with Jack and we were back to before the TAA. To before Raf even. I half-expected Daisy to pop out from behind a panel and have a go at me for quite how dirty and unattractive I looked.

But she didn't. 'Cos she was dead. My face fell again as the present came flooding back in.

'What's going on, Noa?' Jack's voice fought its way through the mess.

'Nothing.' I tried to smile, tried to fix the smile in place.

Jack wasn't fooled. Friends, real friends, know when you need to be silent and when you need to talk, even if you don't know the difference yourself.

'Noa?'

'It's...' My voice faded away.

'Don't say it's nothing. I *know* you.'

'I just keep seeing those people dying. I keep hearing their screams.'

'I know. It was awful. They were butchered. But that's on the Ministry. That's not on you.'

'But you don't understand. It *is* on me. Me is precisely who it's on!'

Jack said nothing but just looked at me with his open face. Every freckle a patient question mark. Waiting. Not judging.

'I told them, Jack,' I whispered. 'Back when me and Raf went to trade at the settlement, I told them we killed the Raiders and then they guessed we were breaking out and that's why they followed us and climbed the Fence and were shot to pieces.' It came out in a rush. My guts spilled in a pile on the floor.

Jack wrapped his arms round me and squeezed.

In a while he spoke again. His voice quiet and thoughtful.

'If they hadn't followed us, if they hadn't climbed the Fence after us, we'd all be dead.'

It didn't come out as a platitude, designed to comfort me, but a statement of fact.

'I've been going over it,' he continued. 'The only reason the soldiers didn't search for us more is that they thought they'd killed everyone. Think about it. If they'd responded to the siren and found a hole in the Fence, do you think they'd have stopped until they found the people? The Fish who'd escaped? Us? The settlers lives weren't in vain. Our mission would have failed without them.'

'But… But…' I stammered. 'How can we claim our lives are more important than theirs? Our mission more important than sixty other people?'

'We can't claim that. I'm not saying that.'

I was about to crumple into myself again when Jack put his hands on my shoulders, pushing them back, squaring out my frame and letting the energy back in.

'You'll get through this. We all will. We've done bad things. We'll probably keep on doing bad things. But the alternative is giving up and we can't give up. Too many people have died to get us where we are. We owe them, Noa. We owe them.'

And then he leant in and planted a single kiss on my lips.

We walked back to camp without talking.

It was as if the kiss hadn't happened.

Jack didn't mention it.

I didn't mention it.

Had I had a weird low blood-sugar moment and just invented the whole thing?

But then I remembered the feel of his lips brushing against mine. The roughness of his chin.

It had happened.

The question was what to do about it.

I tried to rationalise everything. Dissect it as if it was some plotline on a TV show. It wasn't exactly a full-on snog. Our mouths had been totally closed. It was the sort of kiss you might give a friend or a cousin if you came from one of those cool, passionate Latin families where everything is accompanied by hand gestures and drama. But the thing is, I didn't. And Jack certainly didn't. His mum's hands and mouth were surgically attached to a wine glass and moving them around would have risked spilling the precious contents. And if it was just a friendly 'comfort' kiss, why had my heart beat a little faster than normal? It wasn't the crazy fireworks that there'd been for my first kiss with Raf, but maybe nothing's like that first kiss, that first boy. All I knew was that my arms had wanted to wrap themselves around Jack's chest. To feel his solidity. His strength. That can't happen in cool, passionate Latin families every time they kissed a friend or a cousin or they'd be having heart attacks left right and centre and lots of deformed babies as a result of incest.

I kept sneaking side glances at Jack but he seemed undisturbed, normal. Maybe it hadn't meant anything at all to him. Maybe it was some nothing-y rebound thing after Megan. Or maybe, just as bad, maybe he *had* been going to go in for a full-on snog and got put off by something. I pretended to yawn but was really just testing my breath. It seemed fine. Not super grim or anything. I had to think about something else or I was going to scramble my brain. What went well with mushrooms? Garlic. *JACK. YOU KISSED JACK.* Maybe we'd find some wild garlic down another row of panels. *YOU KISSED JACK.* Shut up brain! *YOU KISSED JACK AND YOU CHEATED ON RAF.*

This internal fight – me against my brain – went on like this until we were back at camp. Everyone was awake again and Ella and Lee had returned too. Raf was signalling me over with his eyes, but my feet stayed put. I wasn't ready to face him now. To tell him … I hadn't even thought about what I would or wouldn't tell him. Technically, it wasn't my fault. Jack had kissed me. But I hadn't moved away, had I? And, anyway, this wasn't about technicalities. This wasn't some court of law. This was about Raf and me and him being weird and me screwing everything up.

Nell was a released spring of energy and bounced over to check out our haul and, in an attempt to cover up any weirdness, I started talking weirdly (good one, Noa) in overdrive about finding the mushrooms and how different they all looked and how amazing they all were. Nell looked at me like maybe I'd had a bit too much sun and then started examining the mushrooms, separating them out using a stick.

By now the others were looking on too, drawn by the noise.

'Successful trip?' Raf's voice from the edge. I turned to look at him. Eyes blue and green, but lined with red, shining through dishevelled hair. What had I done? He was wearing a smile but I could see the pain beneath. A bit of me crumbled.

'Very successful, thanks, mate,' Jack replied.

Jack never calls Raf 'mate'. Oh no. Oh no. Please don't let it all kick off.

Ella unwittingly came to the rescue.

'Why are you taking out those ones, Nell?' she asked, pointing at the umbrella mushrooms Nell was putting to one side.

'These ones?' Nell replied with a laugh. 'Back at Ararat we called them Devil Clouds. They're poisonous. Really poisonous. One bite and…' Nell mimed a finger slicing her neck. She may not have had much in the way of schooling, but she knew how to survive, which it turns out is actually far more useful than trigonometry.

Jack and my faces fell. Provider to poisoner in one wrong pluck.

'Noa,' Raf said with a half-grin, channelling wolf but producing injured dog. He was trying to apologise. Trying in every way he knew how. 'Are you and Jack trying to kill me here?'

There's that phrase: hiding in plain sight. It's how famous people go around unnoticed if they just wear a cap and don't have a million bodyguards in sunglasses shadowing their every move. If you see them, you just think – there goes a slightly above averagely attractive short person. I guess that's what the Server was doing, minus the attractive and short bit. The word, the idea –SERVER – had always had this air of mystery, of impenetrability, to it. The place where magical uploads that made other people clever were stored before being winged through the ether to pupils' Scribes, the personal computers they took home with them. (This obviously before I realised the uploads were actually evil brainwashing devices that turned people into robots.) As Megan had confirmed, no one in the

Opposition knew where it was. The Server made you think of high fences, machine-gun towers, a shroud of overgrown brambles and a sleeping princess. But the reality was much more mundane. It was sat on the crest of a minor hill in the middle of a solar field, with a single mast that scratched the sky. Probably no one in the Opposition had found it because no one had come this far or, if they had, they'd thought it was just another squat brick building, nothing special. And that's what the Ministry had been counting on.

We didn't know exactly what we'd be facing. When Ella and Aunty Vicki had been here unintentionally, as a pit stop on their way to the Arable Lands, they'd been found by soldiers here. We couldn't see any now but that could mean that they were inside or it might be that they only station soldiers around the time of the TAA as that's when people try to run. To escape the Cities. We had to assume the worst. Assume there were soldiers. Assume they were watching. We had to view our approach as an attack.

Even when a hill's more mole than mountain, attacking from below leaves you at a disadvantage. Loses you the element of surprise as your enemy can see you coming. To get round this we made the final approach on hands and knees, making sure no body part extended above top of panel height. The earth was rough and loose stones tore through my trousers and grated my knees. I bit my lip but refused to cry out. It felt like some sort of atonement. A punishment I deserved. Cheated on your boyfriend? No problem. Say fifty Hail Marys and then crawl on your hands and knees for an hour and your sin will be washed away. Or rather scraped off.

I'd told Ella what had happened with Jack. I hadn't been able to sleep last night and had gone to sit away from the others. To try and lose myself in the stars. Ella had clearly had the same idea. She took one look at my face and demanded to know everything. I'd told her, hoping for some sympathy, I guess – not that I deserved it – or some advice, but she snapped at me. Told me I should tell Raf. Break up with him. That this wasn't a time for secrets and lies. This wasn't a time for messing around with people's feelings. She might have been right but it didn't make the night pass any faster. Didn't stop my brain from spinning.

Everyone was struggling with the heat. It burned down from above and then bounced off the solar panels, frying us from all directions. Sweat plastered my hair to my forehead and trickled down my legs. We weren't wearing mosquito repellent any more, no longer needing it now that we were on the right side of the mosquito grids, so we didn't have the lavender oil to cover up B.O. And we didn't smell good. Nell wasn't so bad. Maybe because she was younger. Or maybe because she'd never used the oil, we didn't notice as much of a difference.

No one spoke. But that had been pretty much the same all day. Ella had retreated into herself, shutting down more and more with every step towards the Server, towards the place of her mum's death. Her torture and execution. I wasn't talking to Jack and he wasn't exactly seeking me out either. At least he hadn't said anything else to Raf. No more cryptic comments. No more 'mate'. Although this put the emphasis on me to tell him. I'd never thought I'd have to deal with this. Be the baddie. I thought I was a good person. Kind of assumed I'd meet someone special, and be with them for the rest of my life, like Mum and Dad. Agggggghhhhhh! Raf kept trying to get me by myself but I wasn't ready so I was avoiding him. Avoiding my own guilt. Deflecting his whispered apologies.

'I'm so sorry, Noa.'

'I didn't mean it. Any of it.'

'I never meant to hurt you.'

'I'm such a denser.'

'Noa…'

Like he was the only one in the wrong.

I thought I was too tired, too angry at myself to be scared. But as we crawled closer and closer to the Server the now familiar stomach lurch feeling returned. The one that picks up your guts and twists. Performs an internal cat's cradle.

The hum was obvious by now, so distinct. HUMMMMMMMMMM HUMMMMMMMMMM. Pulsing from the Server. A warning. Stay away from the hive.

Another few metres and we could just about see through the windows. There were figures inside. At least three, maybe more. The windows didn't give a clear view of the whole room. And we were looking up at an angle so couldn't see anything below their shoulder height. There could have been a whole army of five-foot guys we would miss entirely. The people we could make out were dressed in grey. They didn't look like normal military outfits but maybe this was some sort of casual Solar Fields version. A bit like the dress-down Friday Dad had at work.

Ella had stopped. She had abandoned crawl position and instead rolled up into a ball. Rocking and chewing her hand. Eyes blank. Lee was about to push her forward when I intervened.

'She stays here,' I hissed. 'She stays outside.'

Lee didn't argue. Something in my expression told him it would have been pointless. And he'd probably worked out that Ella in her current catatonic state would have been less of an asset and more of a liability anyway.

He signalled to our backpacks. We'd agreed this sign already. It meant weapons out. Me and Jack pulled out the hedge trimmers, switching to commando crawl so our hands were off the ground and free to wrap round the metal handles. Lee had his hands and Megan's training and a hunting knife he'd taken from the Raiders' settlement. Raf had a knife too – a stubby, not particularly sharp, short-bladed thing that he'd used for cutting kindling for fires and gutting rabbits. Nell, well, Nell had nothing. The plan had been to leave her at the back, to keep her shielded from the action but she was having none of it.

'I'm going to be armed,' she'd said, a trace of steel to her voice. 'I'm not strong enough to strangle anyone or break anyone's neck and I'm not going to be left, helpless ... with the soldiers...' You could almost watch the thoughts scan across her forehead. One of those paper books where you flip the pages and the little man moves, robot dance style. She'd seen what guys could do. How guys could treat their prisoners. How they could abuse their power.

Lee had been going to argue but Raf stepped in and handed her his own knife. He didn't say anything – just pressed it into her hands with a tiny nod of acknowledgment. A sort of 'I've listened and heard you' nod.

He was a good guy. He might be going through an angry, unpredictable phase and been a bit slow to join in the Nell-in-the-river rescue, but he was still a good guy. I AM A DENSER. Ella was wrong. I shouldn't tell him anything. To tell him would be to lose him and I wasn't ready for that.

We reached the end of the row. There was nothing left to shield us now. Every second we sat and waited was a second in which we could be discovered.

The Server had a single door. A window to the left. Two

windows to the right. Both barred. The door looked pretty serious – all thick studded metal and no glass panel. But that didn't matter. It was open. A foot. Probably to let air in on this scorching day. No reason to lock it with people inside.

Lee pointed at us then straight at the door. 'GO!' his whispered command.

We were on our feet. My legs kept folding underneath me as I ran, the muscles cramped into crawling style for so long they'd forgotten how to operate normally, how to bear weight. My tongue felt abnormally large in my mouth. Like it was pressing into my teeth and the back of my throat. Like it might choke me.

Jack was first through the door. Kicked it properly open and then charged in, trimmers outstretched. A yell of surprise then this horrible sound of slicing and then gargling as one of the guys inside drowned in his own blood. Shouts from another as Lee was next through, followed by a muffled scream and then a simple but sickening 'click'. It was my turn. I ran through the door, hedge trimmers thrust in front. The third guy, there'd only been three after all, had his hands to the side and was edging along a desk that stretched the length of the wall. A desk lined with computer monitors. He wasn't a soldier. Hadn't been trained for combat. He had the sort of hunched frame and super pale skin of Uncle Pete, that comes from never leaving an office. From avoiding all physical work and sunlight. Fear radiated off him in waves. The whites of his eyes so large I could see the veins towards the back of them. Worms in flour. He was talking to me, his voice a high-pitched whine.

'Don't hurt me! Please don't hurt me!'

I was moving forward but I couldn't do it. Hedge trimmers were just a big pair of sharp scissors. I couldn't cut a person up with scissors.

'Noa,' Lee from the edge of the room. 'You need to take him out. Before he sets off an alarm.'

I took another step forward but now I could see the blood vessels leaping in his neck. Vessels I'd have to sever.

His hand was reaching for a drawer. I didn't know what was in the drawer.

'Noa!' Lee's voice again, angry with urgency. I glanced towards him. In that split second, the guy had his hand in the drawer and had pulled out a gun. It was pointed at me.

'Put down your weapon,' the man said, his voice shaking as much as his hands. 'Put it down,' a sort of deranged scream this time.

'Don't listen to him!' Lee shouted.

The man swivelled and aimed at Lee instead. His energy was properly crazy now. Any second and the gun was going to go off.

I could sense someone moving round to my right. Edging towards the guy.

'I'm putting the cutters down,' I said, slowly beginning to lower the cutters to the floor, trying to inject calm into my voice. What other option did I have? He'd shoot me before I could reach him.

I'm not exactly sure what order everything happened in next. Ella's face, slightly dazed, appearing in the doorframe. Raf leaping for the guy and getting him in a chokehold. The gun firing as he span to the left. The scream. Ella's scream as the bullet bit into her flesh. The crumpling sound as Ella's limp body fell to the floor.

'NO!' I sprinted towards her.

There was a hole in the centre of her chest. A rose of blood spreading, blooming. A fountain, pulsing. I pressed my hands over the wound, trying to stop the flow, trying to push the blood back in. It seeped over my palms and trickled through the gaps in my fingers. Her face was so pale, too pale, and her eyes weren't seeing me. Like she was already staring into a different world.

Nell wouldn't approach, just hung back by the door. She didn't want to acknowledge what was happening.

I talked to Ella. Kept up an inane flow of conversation.

About the past. 'Remember that time when you came to stay and we stayed up all night doing rap battles. We were The Rhyme Masters. And you were so much better than me. Remember? "I'm the rhyme master/We're heading for disaster."

About the future. 'We're going to put everything right,

you know. We'll change the system and it'll be a really great place to live again. We'll get a good flat. Live together. I'll help you meet some fit guy. Not that you need help.'

To say sorry. 'I should have killed him, Ella. I shouldn't have panicked. I wish I'd killed him.'

'Noa.' It was Lee's voice, gentle. 'Noa, she's ... she's gone now. Noa…'

But I refused to believe it. I kept talking and kept holding her hand until it went cold.

I closed her eyes and wrapped my jumper round her and pretended she was sleeping. I hope the place, the new place she was seeing, is nice. I hope she meets Daisy there.

The man's body was slumped in a corner, Raf sitting by his feet.

'Is he dead?' I asked flatly. I wanted him to be dead. I wanted it so much.

Raf shook his head. He'd kept up the chokehold until the guy had passed out but hadn't killed him.

'We don't know anything about how things work here. We might need some help.' He said it like an apology.

I didn't react. Didn't know how to. The world wasn't making a whole lot of sense and everything seemed distorted and surreal. Like I was watching it rather than living it. Noa looks concerned. Noa takes a step towards Raf. Raf hugs Noa.

The next thing I knew I was crying. Sobbing into his t-shirt until it was damp and semi see-through. Releasing all the adrenalin I hadn't even been aware had been stored in my body.

'Shh!' he whispered into my hair, rubbing my back, soothing me like you might a baby. 'Shh! I'm always going to protect you.' And then I started blubbing again. A cocktail of love and guilt and fear.

Torture works, that's what the Ministry taught us. It's a horrible, horrible thing that you want to be shielded from, but it gets the information. The ends justify the means. Back in the First City we were always being told about yet another 'evil Opposition plot' to kill babies or something equally horrific that had been foiled using 'heightened interrogation techniques'. Break the subject, crack the code, save the babies.

I should have realised that, like everything else, it was lies. All lies.

I know. We tried it.

The man, the worker, came to after about fifteen

minutes. From unconscious to conscious via a deep rasping intake of breath and a groan. There was already a purplish bruise circling his neck, an amethyst necklace, the colour deepening with time. I looked at it and willed it to hurt. Willed it to squeeze the murdering air out of his murdering throat. Raf had tied the man's hands and feet together so when he tried to stand he only managed to lift himself to kneeling before collapsing down again … thunk … with no means to soften his fall.

Ella's body was outside, still wrapped in my jumper. We would bury her later. First we had to deal with the upload. Deal with the man.

Lee was focused and stressed in a way I'd never seen him. Everything rested on him now. No one else had the skills to hack the system and alter the code. No one else even knew where to start.

He turned on the monitors and perched on this swivel chair, staring intently at lines of code. His mouth closed in concentration, his dark almond eyes a focused beam. Like an extreme version of Dad doing Sudoku.

'Is it an upload?' I asked, my voice hushed, awed by what I didn't understand. A sailor in the olden days looking at the horizon and hoping we weren't about to sail off the edge of the world. I was properly malc at Computer Skills at school, not that we'd gone beyond really basic coding anyway. The more advanced stuff was reserved for the Further Education Schools. For the kids who had passed the TAA. For after the weaklings, the potential Opposition members, had been screened out and shipped off. No surprise there. It was difficult to wrap my head round the fact that Lee had understood it enough to go further independently, far enough to hack into the school computer system in search of more information, true information. Fact to replace fiction. I guess it's a bit like an aptitude for language. Back at the start of junior school when we still did French, some kids just picked it up instantly, embraced it, whereas I never got much beyond BON JAW.

Lee nodded but was still frowning.

'So,' I continued, unwilling to leave his side, 'is there somewhere we just type something like *wake up guys, you've all been brainwashed?*'

Lee laughed. A bark. Harsh. And it was definitely an 'at me' not 'with me' chuckle.

'Sorry,' he replied, icily. 'But it's a bit more complicated than that.'

I didn't take too much offence. I knew I was ignorant. And, more importantly, I knew that the fate of our mission, the fate of the Territory, of everything, now lay in Lee's hands. He moved from terminal to terminal, his frown deepening and deepening, his mouth a Roman road of straightness. His fingers started connecting with the keyboard. This was it. He was doing it. Interpreting the code. Altering it.

'There's no point.' A soft, squeaky voice from the floor. The worker. The killer.

'Ignore him,' from Raf.

Then a few minutes later it came again. 'You're wasting your time.' The voice again was quiet. Not much more than a mumble. Tired rather than goading.

'What? Why's that then?' Lee was on edge, irritable.

'You can't change the uploads. They're digitally signed.'

Lee thumped his fist against the desk. I'd never seen him angry before. Not so angry that he was lashing out, losing control.

'What is it?' I didn't get what was happening. 'What does that mean?'

There was a long pause and Lee showed no signs of answering me. He just stood behind the back of the swivel chair, flexing his hands, before laying them, flat palmed against the plastic. Guess he didn't want to play teacher as everything fell apart.

Instead, Raf filled in the gaps.

'It means the Nodes will reject our upload. If the uploads are digitally signed then the circuitry inside the Node can check to see if the data has been tampered with during its broadcast and if it has, it'll be discarded.'

No one breathed.

Lee's hands were no longer flat, they were gripping the top of the chair, knuckles white where bones pressed against skin.

'Can't we just add the signature ourselves?' I asked, aware really that if it was this simple, Lee wouldn't be looking like he was about to go nuclear.

'We need to know the keys,' Raf explained. 'The strongest digital signatures have two keys – a public key and a private one. The public one sits inside the Node so acts as a sort of lock. That's fine. That's there already. It's the private one that's the issue.'

'How do you even know this stuff?'

'Do you remember when France's nuclear power stations all stopped working and they had virtually no power?'

'Sure. I vaguely think I've heard that. It was crucial to stopping the Western invasion, right?'

'Right. Well that was us. The Ministry. A computer virus with a digital signature discovered through insider knowledge and good old-fashioned spying. Dad told me once, when he was drunk. He was bragging about it. Some friends of his from the Ministry had been involved. I should have thought they might have secured the uploads like this. Should have realised there was a reason the Server wasn't guarded more heavily. Why it didn't need to be. I don't know why I didn't think of it.'

'Doesn't matter,' Lee was forcing confidence into his voice. 'We'll derive the private key from the system here.'

'You can't. The system's been designed by the best. It's impossible.' The squeaky voice again. The worker.

Lee released his grip on the chair but sent it flying across the room as he did so. His eyes were dark flashes. His mouth open, the gap between his teeth a tunnel where bats lived. He turned on the man.

'Where's it stored?'

'In the Ministry.'

'But you know it, don't you?'

'No,' the man's tone was guarded. 'We're not given it. It's patched in by the Ministry before transmission. We don't have it here.'

'Expect us to believe that?' Lee prowled up to the man, who was attempting to stand again, and kicked his legs from under him.

He turned to face us, forced us to meet his eyes.

'This man knows the key to making our upload work. Without this information our plan fails. The freakoids remain brainwashed. The Ministry remains unquestioned. All of our efforts, everyone who's died, it will all be for nothing. We need him to talk. We need to make him talk.'

'I don't know it. I honestly don't.' We ignored the man's protestations. Blocked out the note of desperation in his voice and nodded at Lee. We were with him. The man had lost all his rights when he'd pulled the trigger and killed Ella. If he didn't give us the code, Ella died in vain, Megan died in vain. Those sixty people were gunned down on the Fence for no point whatsoever. The two other workers we'd just taken out. We'd basically murdered them all.

Whatever we did now, it was justified. Whatever we did, we had no choice.

I don't really want to go into what happened next. It makes me feel sick to the stomach. Sick with the world. Sick with us. Sick with myself.

I can't even tell you exactly who did what. We were acting as one. An organism. Someone stamped on the man's hand. Stamped till he cried out in pain.

'I don't know anything.'

Kick to the kidney.

'I don't know anything.'

Kick to the other kidney.

'My name's Fred. Fred Jones. I just work here. We don't get told this stuff.'

Stamp on his head.

It was worse now, now that he had a name. It was easier when he was 'the man'. Easier to hurt the man than Fred. Fred was a person. Fred might have a family. *But Fred killed Ella.*

'Tell us and we'll stop.'

'I don't know anything. I swear I don't know anything.'

Hedge trimmers opened. Glinting in the overhead bulb. Pretty, almost. Like jewellery.

'I'm sssssssorry about your friend. It was an accident. The gun went off. OK. It went off. And … and … you were going to kill me. No, STOP!'

Nine fingers instead of ten.

'I don't know anything. Make it stop. Make it stop.'

Eight.

'OK, OK, I'll tell you. I'll tell you everything. The code, the key it's, it's…'

Stamp to the hand. 'Keep talking.'

'It's in the computer. It's stored in the computer.'

'Where?'

Silence. The man's eyes were darting round the room. There was no unguarded exit. There was no escape.

'Don't hurt me. Please don't hurt me.'

'Where?'

The man's breaths were these shallow pants. Rex in the car on a hot day.

'On the main hard drive?'

'Exactly. Exactly. On the hard drive.'

Lee walked towards the monitors.

The man must have used this distraction to reach for the hedge trimmers as the next thing we knew he'd sliced open his own throat and was bleeding out on the floor. A pool that spread and stained. Scarlet. Viscous.

It was like we'd all been bewitched and his death broke the spell. We stared at the bloody, bruised, mutilated figure on the floor and it was like being sucker punched.

That was us.

We did that.

To another human.

That was us.

'Lee?'

Raf's voice. But it was also all of our voices. A communal prayer. Please have found some information. Please let him have given us some valid information. Please let it have meant something. Please let it have been the only way.

'Nothing.'

Lee's voice was flat. The man had been telling the truth. I could see that now. We all could. He didn't know anything. He'd just made up stuff to make us stop. And then killed himself as the only way out.

The ground was hard and stony and we didn't have proper spades. We'd left them at the Fence so had to use whatever tools we found in the Server building. A wrench. A saw. Two hammers. The old metal side of a computer terminal.

The grave was shallow, no more than a foot deep. We wrapped Ella's body in a tarpaulin we'd found in a cupboard under some spare uniforms and then covered it with earth. When we'd finished it looked more like a mutant molehill than a grave. It was the best we could do but it wasn't enough. Wasn't good enough for my cousin. Wasn't good enough for our friend.

Raf and Jack both tried to comfort me. Tentatively placed hands on my arms. Tried to hook arms round my shoulders. But I shrugged them off. I didn't want the contact. This wasn't about them. This was about Ella. Only Ella. I wanted to lie down and cry. To pummel my feet and hands against the earth and scream. Over and over. To rage against the unfairness of the world that took life indiscriminately. The Greeks got it right. Gods don't love people. People are their pawns and playthings that can be hurt over and over and then left to die. But I knew I had to package my grief. I had to bundle it up and store it away or I'd break, crumble into a hundred pieces, and I couldn't break now. We had to keep going.

Nell couldn't package. She was younger. She'd lost her mother figure. The only 'mum' that had ever cared for her. Loved her. She fought and scratched Jack as we laid Ella in the ground. Bared teeth and nails like a wild thing.

'We need stones,' she kept screaming. 'She won't be at peace without the stones.' I remembered the burial sites in the Wetlands. The mounds of bodies surrounded by concentric circles of white stones that ranged from boulders to large pebbles, topped with bundles of sweet-smelling sea lavender. I hadn't realised that the stones were more than decorative. That a whole mythology had sprung up around them. That they were an offering to the underwater God who guarded the entrance to the Sea of Tranquillity.

There were no white stones in the Solar Fields. None. There were small gravelly stones, bits of orange and brown, uneven and tooth-sized, but nothing with any majesty.

I took Nell's thin, wiry frame into my arms and held her there. Enveloped. Trapped. I told her about Ella's God. About a different version of heaven. Where you didn't need white stones. Where it didn't matter if or how you were buried as long as your conscience was clear and your heart was pure. About how Ella was now at peace and always would be. And as I spoke these words I understood. Understood why, despite the horror, despite the unfairness, or rather because of it, we needed the concept of heaven. That without it death destroyed the living too.

We buried the dead workers down the next row. I don't know who suggested it but it seemed the right thing to do. Not that it made amends or lessened what we'd done.

When we'd finished I headed away from the group into the Solar Fields. Picked up my backpack and walked down a row, crossing into parallel rows, moving until the others were small dots and I could lie down behind a panel and block them out completely. I needed to be by myself. Needed not to be an 'us' any more. I kind of hated 'us'. The trouble is there's still a me and I can't leave me behind. I don't know anything anymore and I'm no longer sure we deserve to win. That we're any better.

We regrouped the next morning after a night apart. A group of flawed humans with soil in their hair and ghosts in their eyes.

I found Raf and pulled him aside.

Deep breath.

'There's something I need to tell you.'

Raf looked surprised by the seriousness of my tone as much as anything. 'What is it? Is everything OK?'

I struggled to keep my focus. Struggled to ignore the way his eyes sparkled with concern, green and blue plunge pools on a hot summer's day, and the way the left-hand corner of his mouth lifted up fractionally higher than the right. But I knew I had to speak. I had to set things straight.

There was only one way to do it.

'That night in the Solar Fields when I went to pick mushrooms with Jack he kissed me.' I rushed out the words before I could chicken out.

A sharp intake of breath and Raf took a step back. Like my words had punched him in the solar plexus.

'You ... kissed ... Jack?'

'He kissed me...'

Raf's shoulders relaxed a fraction, but I knew I had to tell him everything. I couldn't lay all the blame at Jack's feet.

'He kissed me but I didn't pull away. I'm sorry, I should have told you sooner.'

'Why are you even telling me now?' Eyes narrowed to green and blue slits. The sparkle was gone. They were frozen shards of ice. Coloured popsicles that taste of nothing. 'Do you want to be with him? Are you choosing him?'

'No. It's not that. It's that … we're not good people, Raf. We're becoming bad people. What we did yesterday…' I swallowed. Raf swallowed. Trying to swallow images. *Nine. Eight.*

'I don't want there to be any more lies. I want to be a better person.'

I wanted to be someone Ella could be proud of.

'So? That's it? We're over?' I couldn't tell anything from Raf's voice. It was completely flat. Controlled.

I paused.

My mind swung like a malc pendulum clock. Raf the sexy wolf. Raf the massive pain. Having a go at me. Telling me to give him space. Kissing Jack. My heart accelerating. Ella telling me I had to be honest. Had to stop messing people around.

I'd paused too long.

Raf's eyes found the floor. A beat. Then he looked up. Straight at me.

'Well, Noa, I don't want to be with someone who doesn't *know*. That doesn't really do it for me. It's not the *dream I had as a little boy*.' His tone was harsh now, mocking and rising in volume. 'To fall in love with someone, and yes, Noa, I love you – loved you – completely and then have them *not know* how they feel in return! It wasn't supposed to go down that way. So yes, Noa, we're over.'

He span on his heels and started walking back to the group. I willed him to turn and look back. To flash me just one more wolfy grin. To storm back and shout at me. Anything. But he didn't. He kept on going, only stopping briefly to dead arm Jack as he passed.

'What the...!' Jack's yell of outrage.

'She's all yours, *mate*. She's all yours.'

Sometimes doing the right thing sucks. It sucks so bad.

Raf didn't ignore me for the rest of the day. Being ignored would have been better. Shown that he actually cared. Instead he addressed me with perfect courtesy. Deferred to my judgment when we were making decisions. Suggested that I partnered up with Jack.

There was no one to talk to about it all. To spill my heart out to. Nell was barely with it, a nervous mess surgically attached to Jack's arm. I'd never talked about that sort of stuff with Lee, and Ella was gone. Ella. It freaked me out that I could go for a couple of hours without thinking about her. What did this say about me?

I'd seen my cousin killed and I could forget about it. Could still function. After Daisy, I'd been messed up for days. Is death like love? The first time knocks you out and then you start to get used to it. Can you get used to death?

There was one thing we could all agree on. Our next destination.

The First City.

Home.

To hack the uploads we needed the private digital key and the man, Fred – there I did it, I made myself say his name – had said that it was in the Ministry. There was no reason to doubt him and it made sense, too, that the Ministry would retain control over such critical information. There were Ministry branches in all the Cities of course, but the main one, the headquarters, was in the First City. A tall, white building, a flight of steps up to stone columns, a rip off of the Parthenon. No resources to save a few Norms, but enough time and money to give a building an imposing facelift? Sure, why not?

We also knew that if we were going to actually take on the Ministry, enter the lair of the beast if you like, we couldn't do it alone. We needed some help. And the Opposition was based in the First City too. Yin and Yang. Keep your enemy closer.

'You're sure you know how to make contact?' I asked Lee.

'Yes, Megan was really clear about it. She told me the

location of one of their safe houses. Corner of 14th and 7th.'

The north of the City. Not an area I knew well. Our flat, Mum and Dad's rather, was in the west.

'The password's Icarus 34.'

'What?'

'"Cos sometimes you've got to fly too close to the sun",' Lee explained with a wry smile. 'Not sure where the "34" bit came from, though. Anyway, we say the password then we ask for Simon, her brother. He'll help us.'

Everyone started talking about the Opposition. What they knew. How they'd help us.

'...a network of underground tunnels so they can get round the City undetected...'

'... all the latest tech stuff...'

'...a weapons stash...'

It came to me as snippets. I didn't really concentrate on it, past thinking that if the Opposition really was this powerful, how come they haven't already taken down the Ministry? And how come they ever get caught? How did the Ministry find Jack's dad when he was high up in it and *eliminate* him? My mind was elsewhere. I was thinking about home. About Mum and Dad. About whether I could risk trying to visit them and whether they'd even be there. Whether ... whether they'd been taken. How I'd tell them about Ella.

Jack had turned on the TV in the corner of the Server building and my eyes drifted over to my first glimpse of life in the Cities for months. Nothing seemed to have changed. There was some bullshitty propaganda piece about the Head Minister himself visiting the school that had secured the best TAA results last year and meeting (carefully selected) pupils who'd be sitting it next. All the shots were from the front. No back of necks, no Nodes. The message was clear: these pupils work hard, these pupils behave well, these pupils respect the Ministry and that's why they'll pass. A space in the Territory is open to all – all who deserve it. The Head Minister's face stared out at us from the screen. A close-up, designed to impress and reassure. The lighting emphasised his height, his strong jaw, green eyes, grey-flecked brown hair and pronounced chin-dimple. If you didn't know he was an evil autocrat, you might have thought he was a professional rugby player or maybe the charismatic leader of a cult.

Something about him made me shiver, it always had. It was hard to put your finger on it. Objectively he was handsome, in an old-man handsome kind of way, and he looked strong, like he could look after the country. Rower's shoulders Dad used to say. He had no stereotypically cruel features. His mouth was generous, his nose largish but not bulbous, his eyes wide set and often twinkling. But there was something lacking. Some warmth absent. Something that made you suspect the twinkling was electrical, turned on and off by a flick switch rather than by emotion. Not that everyone felt the same way. Lots of people revered him. Genuinely saw him as a kind of Messiah figure. After all, he'd formed the Ministry and led us out of the Dark Days, the horrific violence that had reigned as people fought for land before the building of the Fence and the creation of the TAA. If you didn't have a kid or if you only had Childes, odds on you'd think he was pretty great. If you didn't, and you valued your life and that of your family, odds on you'd be far too scared to tell anyone otherwise or do anything about it.

Behind him stood some lesser ministers. They always seemed to be short, as if chosen to emphasise the Head Minister's height, his superiority. I could just make out Scott, the Minister for Education, squat and bald as if too much learning had stunted his growth and burnt the hair off the top of his head. Next to him stood Cartwright, the Minister for Allocation: small, thin, with glasses, the stereotype of an accountant. Another lackey, all of them the same. Mum said some of them used to be more liberal at the start. That there was lots of heated debate around the TAA. If that was ever true, it no longer is now. Thompson, Khan, Riley, Heywood. It was hardly worth learning their names. Same opinions, same disguised cruelty, same total disregard for teenage life.

I couldn't take it any more so I switched the TV off and turned my attention to Raf and Lee who were now discussing our route.

'If we retrace our steps through the Solar Fields, keeping close to the Fence, we'll minimise our chances of being seen.'

'Then cut inland through the Woods?'

'But that will add about two days of walking.'

'It's better than being spotted.'

Jack joined in, 'And what about when we get to the First City? We look like vagrants. I mean look at us?'

I looked from face to face, scanning head to toe. Trying to view us objectively rather than relatively. Like a random passer-by who lived in the Territory and had daily access to showers might. God, we looked awful! Dirty in a way that a good wash in a stream couldn't sort out. Knees and elbows peered out of ripped clothes, the guys' stubble had sprouted into proto beards, and everyone's hair was an out-of-control matted mess. We were a walking Have You Seen Anything Suspicious? poster. And there was Nell. Nell was another thing entirely. Her gleaming white skin and white hair would freak people out immediately. We'd got used to it but I remember when me and Raf first saw Cara, the Cell at the Peak. We couldn't help but remark on it, share the news about the strange-looking bleached girl.

'Jack's right,' I said, defeat lowering and flattening my voice. 'We'll be spotted immediately. Arrested immediately. If we even get that far. There are soldiers patrolling the edges, the Woods, probably even the Solar Fields. When they find out someone's attacked the Server then patrols will double, triple. Everyone will be looking for us. We can't count on getting past them all, whatever route we take.'

'So, we arm ourselves and take our chances?' Lee's tone was grim. He didn't reckon on our chances either but what choice did we have?

I scanned my brain for ideas. There must be something. Scan scan – Nothing – *I'm really hungry*. Scan scan – Nothing – Scan scan – *Ping*! There it was. There was something we could do.

'The uniforms! That's it. Remember the cupboard I got the tarpaulin from? Yes? Well, above it were spare uniforms. Uniforms for the workers here. Not like the casual dress-down ones we saw them in but real hard-core soldier uniforms! Probably for inspections or high-up visitors or something. People won't stop us if they think we're soldiers. Not if we walk straight enough, yell loud enough. Not if we style it out right.'

My speech was a garbled mess but it didn't matter, everyone started nodding anyway. We'd do it. It was ballsy. Confidence was key. We were going to be like the guys in a heist film who walk into a building wearing hi-vis jackets claiming they are there to test the alarm. I blocked the fact that now in Ministry-allowed films those guys always got caught. Anyone who tried anything remotely against the system, even on celluloid, got caught. And killed.

I bounded over to the cupboard and started chucking out uniforms – biggest to Jack, smallest to Nell. We undressed and pulled them on, smoothing down creases, tightening belts, tucking hair into berets. Nell had to roll the bottom of her trousers up a couple of times and there was a gap between the top of Jack's socks and the trouser hem but apart from that they fitted OK. The shirt, trousers, beret combo meant that Nell's hair was tucked out of sight and only her face and neck were exposed so she could probably pass as a girl who just happened to have very pale skin. There was a triumphant yell from the bathroom and Lee ushered us in to reveal a stash of toiletries, soap, toothbrushes, razors he'd found in a drawer. We set to work – washing, scrubbing, the guys shaving – their newly smooth chins looking strangely naked and vulnerable. The skin there was paler than on the rest of their faces, having been hidden from the sun for a couple of months.

We stood in front of the bathroom mirror and surveyed the results.

It was weird. Stomach-flip level weird seeing us like this. Dressed as the enemy. Like pretending to be a witch at Halloween if witches were actually real and actually built candy houses to lure kids in to eat them. The disguise wasn't perfect. Not by any means but maybe good enough. And, as we weren't planning to get too up close to anyone, good enough would have to do.

As a final measure we raided their food store and filled packs with Mucor bars and bottles of water.

I was almost beginning to enjoy myself when Raf came over.

'Good idea of yours, Noa.'

And that was it. A compliment. Genuine. But nothing more. No compliment plus joke. No compliment plus grin. And the missing plus, the difference between Noa and Raf, girlfriend and boyfriend, partners in crime, and Noa and Raf, polite acquaintances, was a stab to the chest. A knife left in the ribcage and twisted.

I reckon we're about another two days' walk from the First City. Three days down, two to go. We're covering ground faster than ever. Out of the Solar Fields, through the Woods and skirting the edge of the Third City. We're not stopping much. Short, efficient breaks but no long group chats. Raf occasionally needs to stop for longer if he gets one of his headaches but he won't let me comfort him, check on him even. His flat eyes a 'no-entry' sign. I'll sometimes see him huddled with Lee. Telling him stuff. Me, no, never.

Everyone's still in their own heads a lot. Thinking about what has been and what is lying ahead. Thinking about Ella. Mourning her. I hadn't realised what a stabilising influence she'd been on the group. She was friends with everyone (well, apart from Raf) and she'd been a kind of centre point between me and Raf on one side and Jack on the other. The pivot in a moment's calculation gone.

Everything's still really awkward between me, Raf and Jack. This morning Jack kept trying to walk next to me, like I was some bone that Raf had dropped and was now his to claim, whereas Raf couldn't bear being next to me and would slow down or speed up to make sure it never happened.

We're also sticking to the paths and roads which makes marching easier. One stride on tarmac/intentionally flattened and cleared dirt track equals about three little steps over brambles or five hops from stone to stone across a stream. Lee's still worried about our hiding in plain sight plan. He'd have preferred us to try to stay properly hidden. To stick to ditches, to head deeper into the Woods amongst the shrubs and brambles. But I figured that in the army uniforms that would only increase our suspicious rating. Five soldiers marching purposefully along a marked path looks like a small planned manoeuvre. Soldiers moving base. Soldiers chasing a fugitive. Soldiers relaying an important message. Something people could register, accept and then walk away from. Whereas five people in uniform creeping around the undergrowth, bobbing up and down and popping out from behind trees *was* something to notice. Something to report.

Lunch started off well but turned sour.

We stopped near a stream to refill our water bottles and rest our legs.

Not knowing where we'd get our next supplies from, we

had to ration what we had, so lunch was a single Mucor bar. Raf took his and wandered off, probably in search of his ever-needed 'space'.

The Mucor bars were 'Pork' flavour. Yeah right. A few spliced pig cells does not a sausage make. Nell's expression as she took her first bite was hilarious. Her face twisted and her lips puckered like a closing drawstring bag. You could see the battle between her taste buds and her brain as it instructed her oesophagus to swallow. *Peristalise goddamit*! Or whatever the verb for do peristalsis is. Maybe there isn't even a verb.

'What is this stuff?!' she spluttered as soon as her mouth was empty of the offending bite. 'People in the Territory actually like this stuff?!'

If you had a school project to record an example of someone acting incredulous, that would have got a hundred per cent.

'No one likes it,' I replied, trying to get my laughter under control. 'But it's good for you. And *efficiently produced*,' I added, mimicking the catchphrase of the biggest Mucor producer. You know something is going to taste super grim if the best thing they can say about it is that the production is pretty damn efficient.

'But what is it?' Nell still couldn't get over it.

'Fungus.'

'So mushrooms?'

'Kind of. A single-celled fungus grown in a vat that's

had lots of other creatures' genes spliced into it so it generates more protein and vitamins than normal and tastes a bit like meat.'

'What's spliced?'

I hadn't realised how little Nell knew about the Territory, about life here. Not that it should have surprised me. She'd always lived in the Wetlands and hadn't been around this sort of technology.

I tried to explain simply but not patronisingly. 'Splicing involves taking a gene from one organism and inserting it into another organism's DNA.'

'What's a gene?'

'It's a little bit of your DNA – the code that makes you you, or a big brown horse a big brown horse. It has instructions in it that determine what a bit of you looks like, or what your body can do. So you have a gene for eye colour, a gene for making a particular hormone, a gene for being tall. Stuff like that.'

'And they can stick that into a different person or some completely different animal?'

'Yup.'

'Freaky.' Nell shivered.

'Freaky,' I agreed.

Nell's extreme reaction to Mucor managed to lighten the mood a bit so everyone was finally talking and de-stressing slightly as we went to refill our water bottles.

'Noa?' Jack nudged my arm and nodded to the left. He

started to walk upstream, away from the others, and I followed him. He didn't stop until we'd passed a boulder and were semi-screened from the others. Together we peered into the stream. Together. A sensation that was both alien and familiar. Like stumbling across your home in a parallel universe.

The water in the stream was still clear and, judging by the number of creatures skating its surface and hiding in its depths, disease free. I saw a flash of silver and as I leaned forward to see if there really was a fish in the reeds, I lost my footing. Feet skidding down the muddy bank, arms windmilling, my fall was stopped just in time by Jack scooping his arm round my waist. My hands grabbed round his neck for safety. We must have looked like some weird dance partners going for a dramatic finale to their routine. Jack stared down at me with this new kind of intensity.

'Now, how are you going to thank me?' he said, his skin reddening slightly.

I tried to keep things light. Tried to ignore the feeling of his arms.

'Um, how about, "Thanks, kind Sir"?'

'Nope, that's not what I'm looking for,' he replied and dangled me back over the river, upside down so the ends of my hair were trailing in the water.

'Put me down!' I yelled, well, laugh-yelled.

He lowered me further. The base of my skull cradling

the water's surface. The cold stung and made me break into giggles again.

Then slowly, ever so slowly, Jack began to pull me upright again, towards him. The water from my wet hair was seeping into my shirt, making it cling to my skin, and I suddenly felt exposed.

He was moving towards me as well as pulling me towards him. Leaning in. He was going to kiss me again. Oh God, Jack was going to kiss me again.

Crack, snap.

A twig, breaking. I looked up, away from Jack's eyes and towards the sound. There, just higher up the hill, next to a fallen tree was Raf. Starting to move away but staring. That was where he'd disappeared to. I hadn't seen him. We'd focused on the others. Screening ourselves from them. Raf must have been there the whole time. Must have seen us, seen everything. I froze, pliant to rigid in one second.

'What's wrong?' Jack's eyes followed mine and landed on Raf. The three of us, frozen, staring, trapped in the moment.

'Time to go!' came Lee's voice from upstream. The spell was broken but nothing was fixed. We walked back to join the others in silence, our boots clinking along the flint path.

I've always been malc at acting. Shockingly terrible. I was probably the only kid who was pleased when they dropped drama from the syllabus in Year 8. Well, to be fair Jack was pretty happy too. He sucked almost as much as me. Improvisation was the worst. There was this one exercise we had to do in the first year of Hollets. You had to stand in a circle. It would start off with two people in the middle acting out a scene 'of their choice' and then every time Mrs Aster, the drama teacher, rang a bell, they'd freeze and some other poor sucker would have to enter the circle and take the improvisation in a different direction, based on the position in which the central peeps had frozen. I used to stand there, at the edge, deliberately avoiding the teacher's eye, studying windows, the grain and knots of the wooden floor, hoping to God she wouldn't pick me. I remember once when she rang the bell; she called out my name and I was jostled into the centre and just froze. My mind went blank and I couldn't think of anything. There were seven people by now in the centre, all frozen in weird rigid robot poses and I was just standing there opening and closing my mouth and willing my brain to turn on.

Mrs Aster said, 'Any day now, Noa,' in this super-condescending voice of hers and people started to snigger.

That horrible hyena-pack laugh when a group's identified a weak loser and is going to tear them to pieces. Daisy saved me that time. She was one of the frozen ones and she just unfroze (totally against the rules) and pretended to offer me a tour of a waxwork museum, being really rude about the other kids who were still in statue mode, deflecting the attention and laughter away from me. She got a detention but she said it was worth it.

Daisy wasn't there to save us today.

We came across the group of soldiers, a platoon – is that the right word? – soon after breakfast. Nine of them. Marching our way, all in step. Trained soldiers. Disciplined. On a mission. The ground was flat and the path straight so we had a few minutes warning of their arrival. A few minutes to arrange ourselves as a marching column, to straighten our uniforms, to mirror their upright postures.

'What do we do?' hissed Nell from the back. The less people saw of her and her skin the better.

'We walk straight past them,' Lee replied. 'Say nothing, just march. Don't act nervous. We're soldiers on manoeuvre. Nothing more.' He took the lead.

Left right. Left right.

They drew closer and closer.

I hadn't counted on this. I'd thought maybe we'd see people a few roads away, or they'd glance at us from a window, eyes framed by curtains. Not like this. Not face to face. Not soldiers who knew what real soldiers should look and act like. We couldn't flee, they'd easily catch us and they outnumbered us so we couldn't fight our way out. We had no choice. We had to chance it. We had to improvise.

Left right. Left right.

Soldiers look ahead. Soldiers don't fiddle. Soldiers don't hold hands for support or chew their nails. I forced my eyes forwards, imagining a clamp holding my head in position. Strings moving my straightened arms.

Left right. Left right.

'And, Halt!' At their leader's command, the approaching soldiers stopped.

Their direct stares showed they clearly expected us to do the same.

Lee stopped and we tried not to collide into the back of each other.

Their commander stepped forward.

'Group Twelve of the Fourteenth,' his voice was clear and clipped. Proper military.

There was a pause. He was waiting for us to identify ourselves. This must be some standard military procedure. In my head I could hear Mrs Aster's bell ring.

I stared at Lee but he didn't open his mouth. He'd gone pale. He'd frozen. If someone didn't speak soon we were done for. We might as well be holding up a sign saying 'fugitives in fancy dress'.

I looked at Raf but his eyes were distant, clouded with pain. At Jack – his skin was slowly reddening. At Nell – they wouldn't believe a twelve-year-old was in charge.

'Group Nine of the Twelfth,' I said, stepping forward, my mouth deciding to act before I'd even realised my brain had committed. Nine and twelve seemed safe-enough numbers. Close enough to his ones to suggest such a group might exist. I enunciated like I've never enunciated before. *How Now Brown Cow.* And Dad once said something like eighty per cent of communication is body language so I willed every cell in my body to exude arrogance. To adopt an 'I took ages to reply because you're so beneath me' pose. Their commander still didn't look convinced. He'd seen straight through me. My chest was constricting, my throat a straw – one of those ones with valves at the end that are incredibly hard to suck through. I caught his eyes looking me up and down. Not *at* my uniform looking. *Under* my uniform. Maybe he hadn't made me at all – maybe it was a gender thing – maybe he just didn't like women being in charge. Maybe I just had to make him respect me – try and alpha dog him – like those guys who try and exert power through lame-ass 'dominant' handshakes. Jack's step-dad used to do that. Take your hand and then, mid shake, not so subtly twist it over so it was palm side up. Loser. I didn't think soldiers shook hands so I went for the controlling-by-words option.

'State your mission soldier.' I think this was the first time I've ever sneered.

'I thought Saunders ran Group Nine?' Suspicion flickered in the commander's eyes and panic flooded me.

We're screwed. We're totally screwed.

'He's been transferred to Group Seven,' I replied as confidently as I could, praying that there was a Group Seven and that I was only flinching on the inside. 'And your mission, soldier?'

A beat and then he replied. His tone wasn't deferential but it had lost its suspicion, lost its disdain. Consider yourself dominated, sucker!

'There has been an attack on the Server. Nasty business. We're sweeping for fugitives. These Opposition bastards always return to their burrows at some point. And you?'

'Same story,' my voice semi-cracked from nerves so I had to force it to normalise again. 'We were part of the initial response unit but now have orders to return to the Third City. Possible attack rumoured.'

'Well, Good hunting.'

'And you.'

And that was it. Their leader called his gang to attention and they marched off, heading north, towards the Server. I copied his commands, his tone, as I ordered our gang off too, continuing south, the distance between us widening with every hup-to. My legs were weak and my head light – like my brain had been removed, spliced with candyfloss, then replaced. We'd passed. We'd somehow managed to get through it. I'd somehow managed to get through it. Take that, Mrs Aster.

We didn't talk or stop until we'd turned a corner, crossed a bridge and entered what must have been an industrial zone. The road was flanked with Mucor factory after Mucor factory interspersed with the odd algal farm plant and water store. I reckoned we'd put well over three miles between us and the soldiers. Three miles would have to do. The next time a wave of exhaustion hit I succumbed. My legs buckled underneath me and I collapsed to the floor. As I began to let go, all my muscles started convulsing, my teeth chattering in my jaw and my left eyeball vibrating in its socket, tiny bubbles forming at the tear duct. Pop, pop, pop.

I could hardly register Lee and Nell thanking me, their noise, their congratulations reaching my ears as a non-specific, distorted buzz. I think Jack may have hugged me and Raf pulled a facial expression that might have been a grin but could just as easily have been a grimace. I was too tired to tell or care.

A few minutes later Lee was already trying to move us on.

'We need to keep going,' he instructed. 'We haven't covered enough ground. We need to get another five miles in before we make camp.'

Jack and Nell groaned, but started to shoulder their packs, when Raf stood up and blocked their path.

'Absolutely not,' he stated. 'Look at Noa. I mean look at her.' Four pairs of eyes swivelled in my direction. 'She's exhausted. She's shaking. She put herself out there for us. She broke herself for us. The factory we just passed had outbuildings. They looked like they were for storage. Filled with bags not people. We can sleep there tonight and move on tomorrow at first light.'

I was so grateful to him just then. He was right, I couldn't keep going, it would break me. And he knew it. Saw it. Saw me. His certainty, coupled with my zombified face, was enough to convince everyone. Jack carried my pack sheepishly and for once Raf didn't adjust his pace to take himself out of step with me.

'Thanks,' I smiled weakly at him. 'I don't think I could have gone much further.'

'No, thank you,' Raf replied, the corner of his mouth twitching. 'I didn't know you had it in you. When you started to speak I did kind of think – oh no, we're done for!'

'Great, thanks for the vote of confidence!'

'You're welcome. *State your mission, soldier!*' He mimicked my voice but made it all high pitched and wavering.

'It was better than that!'

'State your mission, soldier!' even higher this time, almost warbling.

'Oi!' I went to punch his arm and, out of habit ended

up wrapped round him, gazing up at his face, at his mouth.

Raf tensed.

And then I tensed.

We both tensed and moved apart.

Just as I thought there was a new bridge between us, it turns out it was just one of those flimsy-looking rope ones with rotten slats that swing over canyons, one wrong step and you're a smashed-up mess on the valley floor below.

I've worked it out. We've only been away for three months. It was probably three months exactly since I hugged Mum and Dad goodbye and climbed underneath a prisoner transport truck bound for the Wetlands. Three months can seem like a lifetime.

My skin started to crawl as soon as we saw the towers and high rises of the First City in the distance, rising above the sprawl of the factories and workshops that we had started to work our way through. Knowing that nestled amongst them were Mum and Dad, the Ministry and the Opposition. The good, the bad and the unknown. Suddenly everything seemed pretty hopeless. In the Wetlands it was easier to believe we could triumph. A land where the settlements were small, with never more than a hundred people in any one place, where the buildings were shacks made of corrugated iron sheets and salvaged wood. Easier to believe you could succeed in a place where you could name every individual and kick down the doors and tear apart the buildings with your bare hands. Here things were different. Each block of flats contained over a hundred people, everything was steel and concrete and glass, our targets were protected by heavy security and our every step from now on would be caught by and analysed on CCTV. If the Opposition hadn't managed to change things, how the hell would we?

We were entering the residential zone. The plan was to march close to the safe house and then one of us would slip to the door, knock and give the secret code. Until then we had to keep up appearances, march confidently but with our eyes down and berets pulled forward. It was difficult, virtually impossible, to recognise a person if you couldn't see their eyes, the top half of their face. Me and Raf would be on some list, we were bound to be. The Ministry wouldn't let two people go AWOL without taking action. As soon as we hadn't turned up at Greenhaven when we were supposed to, the photos from our ID cards would no doubt have been uploaded onto a 'search and locate' list, CCTV images being constantly scanned by people with weirdly excellent facial recognition skills.

I'd never been this far to the north in the First City

before. Never been past the outer ring of offices, past the canals, to the flats that were crumbling. Walls that had been graffitied and then painted over, the offending comments still shining through. *Ministry Scum. Kid Killers.* Rats scuttled out of and into holes in the brick like they owned the place, our presence a minor irritation, nothing more. And people's faces were blank, devoid of hope. Paper masks with nothing inside.

I hadn't really ever thought that I lived in a nice part of town. In a nice flat. It was just where I lived. Where my friends lived. OK, the land around Aunty Vicki's was worse than here – grey, salty – but her house was decent. This was different. Almost worse than the Wetlands somehow. Because in the Wetlands everyone was in the same position. You lived in a shack, but everyone lived in a shack. You wore rags and were permanently hungry, but everyone wore rags and was permanently hungry. You'd probably die from malaria but everyone would probably die from malaria.

'Noa?' Lee's voice. I hadn't even realised I'd stopped marching. 'Come on, we have to keep in step or we're not going to fool anyone.'

I apologised and got back in line. Synchronised my steps once more. Dragged my eyes away from the bricks and the rats and the windows with papered-over panes.

The deeper we got into the residential district, the more attention we started attracting. Eyes followed us from behind windows. People crossed the street to avoid us, careful not to make eye contact. You could almost feel, almost smell, the emotions being radiated, they were so strong. An aftershave of fear and hate directed at us and what we represented. I wanted to tell people that we weren't actually soldiers. That we weren't Ministry stooges. That we were trying to make everything better, but of course I couldn't. I had to keep marching. Look like I owned the uniform, wore it with pride.

We were a block away from the safe house when we turned off the main road. The streets here were narrower, enclosed by high buildings and eyes that we could feel if not see. We lurked at a corner, on the left, heads down. We'd chosen the position as it gave us a good view of the radial streets. Plenty of exits in case we needed them. We couldn't see a camera but there was probably one there. Hidden. Watching.

Lee said he'd be back in ten. That we should wait here.

Sting.

'Ow!'

And again.

'OW!'

First my shoulder. Then my right ear. We were being pelted with tiny missiles from above. Bits of stone, a broken pencil, a toothpaste top. Launched from an upstairs window, gaining momentum and force. If one hit our skulls it could do proper damage.

'Quick, this way,' Jack pulled me away from the corner, down an alley to the left. Raf and Nell followed close behind.

The missiles, however, continued, following us from window to window. Our assailants were good; they knew what they were doing. You couldn't predict where the next attack would come from. Unless you looked up for faces behind the glass and looking up was the one thing we couldn't do.

We stopped halfway down the alley under some scaffolding, the wooden boards sheltering us. Just as we were congratulating ourselves, we saw them coming, a dozen figures in black balaclavas carrying cruel-looking wooden baseball bats. Six from the right and six from the left. We'd completely played into their hands. We were surrounded.

The balaclavas masked all facial features except their eyes. But eyes register every emotion; they're windows to the soul and these souls hated us.

They kept on coming.

I saw a bat rise. I saw it swing. Then blackness.

I didn't know how long I was out for. All I knew was that I'd been unconscious and was now awake again. And somewhere new. My senses returned one by one. Touch – first the throbbing pain in my head and ribcage; then my fingertips tracing worn wooden floorboards instead of cold pavement slabs. Hearing – voices, distorted at first then becoming clearer, like someone was adjusting a dial inside my ear. Soft moaning. Harsher fragments of questions. Shrapnel fired from a mouth I couldn't see. Sight – nothing. I couldn't see. I couldn't see anything. I opened my eyes, strained them in their sockets, but still blackness. They've blinded me, they've blinded me. The panic was at the top of my throat and squeezing. My breaths turned to shallow gulps. In. Out. In. Out. On the third breath I felt something brush against my lips and suck into my mouth. Fabric.

Thank God. Thank you, God! I wasn't blind – they'd put a bag over my head, that was all. I don't think anyone in the history of the world has ever been so pleased to have a bag over their head.

I let out a weird, witchy cackle of relief and the next thing I knew, the bag was wrenched off and I was squinting up at a guy whose mouth was open, yelling at me to be quiet. Ironic really. But things like that are never ironic at the time. They're just really frickin' scary. I tried not to show fear. To hide it and find something else to focus on – his teeth. This guy had really small teeth, like milk teeth in an adult mouth – seriously, he'd never have to floss, the gaps between them were so big.

'Noa, is that you?' Raf's voice. Thick with concern. He was worried about me! He cared! I quickly scanned the room. Jack and Nell sat against the far wall, bags still tightly secured over their heads. Raf in one corner, his head covered too. Lee slumped in the other. It didn't compute. How had they got him as well? Did they pick him off on the way to the safe house? Lee's head was exposed and what I saw made my neck whip back in horror. Half of his face was swollen as if he'd had some horrific allergic reaction, like when Sam Hinkley ate a cobnut in Year 4 and his face swelled up to twice its usual size. He had to be taken off in an ambulance. He never came back. Lee's left eye was glued shut and his hair was matted against his forehead. Matted red.

I wanted to go to him, to bathe the blood out of his hair, but one look at the two guys and a girl standing to attention round the room told me that this was not an option.

The Ministry had found us. Maybe they'd known all along. That commander I'd spoken to must have worked it out, seen straight through my malc acting, and then they'd toyed with us – cat and mouse – hoping we'd lead them to an Opposition base. It was all over.

'Let's try again, shall we?' Milk Teeth hissed. 'Maybe a girl this time. People always say that girls are great communicators!'

Heh heh heh. His three pathetic lackeys tittered at his non-joke.

Milk Teeth stalked over to me, shoved a hand under my arm and yanked me up to standing.

'So, how did you find us?' His voice was one-part venom, two-parts testosterone.

'I don't understand?' I answered, surprised but trying to keep my tone neutral, polite. 'You found us.'

This was clearly not the right answer. He kicked my side and a bullet of pain ricocheted up my body. I dropped to my knees. Prayer position.

'Don't lie to me. That's the first rule, OK? Rule numero uno. DO NOT LIE TO ME.'

I was going to be sick. I was being attacked by a crazy Ministry interrogator and I was going to be sick. Was this karma? Was this divine payback? We'd tortured a man and now it was our turn? Eye for an eye. Tooth for a tooth.

'So, again, how did you find us?'

My silence earned me a slap to my face. Cheek hit teeth and ripped open.

Raf and Jack both shouted out and tried to stand but were knocked back down.

'This is nothing, little girl. This is me flirting. You don't want to see me serious. Your friend here,' he pointed at Lee, 'came to our door, asking for Simon.'

A smile spread over my face and my muscles unknotted themselves. This guy wasn't Ministry. He was Opposition. It was all a terrible mistake. Lee must have forgotten the password.

'What are you smiling about?' Milk Teeth's voice was dangerously quiet now. Little more than a murmur.

'Icarus 34,' I said as loudly as I could and then repeated it, volume maxed for luck as a kind of victory lap: 'ICARUS 34!' In my head a pair of oversized cymbals crashed and an imaginary orchestra reached crescendo. *Abracadabra, open the door to the cave full of jewels.* We would all laugh. He'd apologise. We'd graciously accept. Love and war and all that.

SLAP! The back of his hand hit my other cheek. It went numb. I could feel nothing for six seconds and then this terrible burning sensation spread across my face.

'Wrong password!' Milk Teeth shot back. 'I'm telling you, like I told him, your information is out of date. Get a better snitch next time, soldier scum!'

'But Megan...' I started, but couldn't continue as the air was knocked out of my ribcage by another punch.

'Noa, it's no use. I've tried explaining, but he won't listen.' Lee from the corner. His voice, like his body, broken.

Milk Teeth raised his boot again and I braced myself for impact, when the door burst open and another man, older, tall and wiry with grey-streaked hair and a short mottled beard entered.

'Any luck with the prisoners?' Silver Fox asked.

'No. But I'll break them. I'll find the leak,' Milk Teeth boasted.

'No, this is taking too long. I'll take it from here.'

Milk Teeth tensed up before nodding and retreating to the wall. He didn't like it, but he did it. Silver Fox was clearly in charge. He pulled two chairs into the centre of the room and placed a black tool roll on one and began untying and unrolling it. Slowly, calmly – this was an everyday business event for him. Bread and butter work. Like he was attending some regional managers' sales meeting and was about to demonstrate the superior suction power of the VAC3000. Every cell in my body screamed run. Run. NOW. But there was nowhere to go. I shrank into myself and stared at the floor. Tried to make myself look as small and insignificant as possible. Kept my eyes from the chair and the glinting silver instruments shining on it. Examined the boards and focused on the tiny ant that was weaving its way round my feet. Willed my consciousness to jump into its body and scuttle away under the door. As if reading my mind, Silver Fox reached forward and squashed the ant with his right index finger.

'And what did I say about girls?' boss guy continued, taking hold of my chin, turning it through a 180-degree arc, anger finally infecting his voice. 'Not their faces. The Ministry won't exchange her for a comrade if you mess up her face. They've got a thing about it.'

'Sorry, boss.'

Silver Fox stepped away from me and I breathed, pinpricks of tears forming in the corners of my eyes and leaking down my face.

I knew this wasn't it, though. It wasn't going to end just like that. Silver Fox wanted information and was damn sure he was going to get it.

'Bring me that boy over there.' He pointed to the far wall. To Jack.

'No!' I screamed. I couldn't let this happen again. Couldn't let Jack take the fall for me again. 'There's no leak. Listen to me. Megan…' a sweaty palm was clapped over my mouth. This was like the Server all over again. Except this time we were on the other side.

Jack was prodded and then walked over by himself, hands in front, groping at the darkness.

I couldn't do anything.

'It's better this way, Noa,' Jack said, hoping I'd hear him. My good, strong Jack, wanting to take my place.

Silver Fox reached forward and pulled the bag off Jack's head. I closed my eyes, waiting for the first blow to fall.

There was silence. Taut, crackling silence. The kind you can see and feel.

Then Silver Fox spoke, a single, staccato word.

'Jack?'

'Dad?' came the strangled reply.

Jack's dad isn't dead.

Jack's dad isn't dead.

It doesn't matter how many times I say it, it still doesn't seem real.

It is, though, real that is. And now it seems absurd that I didn't recognise him immediately, as soon as he walked into the room.

OK, I hadn't seen him since I was seven and there've been some significant changes since then. He's about ten kilos lighter than the Jack's dad of old, his skin is now creased and furrowed and his hair is more grey than red. However, the fundamentals haven't altered.

Same slightly hooked nose.

Same grey eyes flecked with yellow that should be striking but end up just looking cold.

Same full mouth that straddles the line between passion and cruelty (but a slightly saggier version).

I think I would have recognised him sooner if it hadn't been for the context. Context is everything. They've done experiments on it. Made people watch uberly good sports teams play indoor matches in poor lighting with rubbishy seats and no one could tell that they were any better than the local amateur squads 'cos they weren't expecting them to be. OK, it's a pretty different scenario, but in the storage locker of my brain, Jack's dad was someone who used to pass the cereal at the breakfast table, someone who would shoot his mouth off at something the Ministry had done, someone who was kicked out by Jack's mum, and – here comes the biggie – someone who was *DEAD*. Not someone who prowled underground chambers ordering around psycho thugs and unrolling torture instruments.

Jack, totally understandably, can't seem to wrap his head round it either and appears to be going through something slightly like a stages of grief thing.

Stage 1: denial

He can't be alive. He is but he can't be. Like a corpse that's been exhumed and resurrected. Of course there hadn't been a corpse. Or a funeral. Jack's dad just didn't return to his house one day. Didn't turn up to pick Jack up on one of his appointed visitation Tuesdays. That night there'd been a picture of him on the news as one of a number of 'evil' Opposition members that had been picked up in a 'brave' Ministry swoop to prevent some atrocity. I never learnt what. Dad turned off the TV as soon as he'd seen the photo and Jack never spoke of it. Never. What I did know was that Jack's dad was going to be 'eliminated'. Shot. 'Thank God I left him when I did,' had been Jack's mum's response. That had been Jack's truth for the past eight years and no one had doubted it for a minute.

Stage 2: euphoria

Jack had a dad at last and all his not-having-a-dad issues evaporated like a puddle at noon. After a staring, open-mouthed standoff, (blink first, I dare you) they'd hugged and embraced. Silver Fox a.k.a. Jack's dad explained how he'd escaped Ministry custody and then gone underground, turning the Opposition into a more organised, efficient weapon of dissent. Jack told his dad how we'd battled our way through the Wetlands, destroyed the Raiders, attacked the Server and of our plans to hack the Childe uploads. It was like witnessing the inaugural meeting of a competitive mutual appreciation society. *You're amazing. No, you are. Well, you're better...*

Then Jack's dad took us upstairs, to the kitchen at the top of the building to be fed and showed us to the bathrooms and our sleeping quarters – a series of dorms – introducing everyone we met along the way to 'his son'. Jack's chest was puffed so full it was like it'd been attached to an automatic bike pump. Dinner was followed by showers. Actual hot showers. Getting clean, properly clean. Then to real beds. Mattresses. Sheets. After three months of sleeping on the ground, lying on them felt like the greatest luxury imaginable. I now get why Rex always tried to sleep at the end of mine, no matter how many times I pushed him off. The floor sucks. Beds rock.

Nell couldn't wrap her head around the lights, well electricity in general. OK, she'd seen it briefly at the

Server, but then none of us were in any state to process anything. And I guess if you've never been up close with it before it must look like a cross between a miracle and some kind of dark magic. Even for us who'd grown up with it, three months' absence restored our wonder. A fireless oven. Staying up later than the sun. Nell sat or rather squatted next to the light switch – lights on – lights off – her mouth an open 'O' of wonder. I had to drag her away before she fused the system.

Stage 3: anger and despair

Being introduced to Simon was the tipping point. He came into the living area just as everyone was finishing eating. You just had to look at him to know that he was Megan's brother. Same colouring. Same cheekbones. But more importantly, the same energy – the same slightly wild, dangerous edge. A blade that should be stored on the top shelf, out of reach of kids. Both me and Lee had told Jack we'd break the news of Megan's death to Simon, that there was no reason he had to put himself through it, but Jack insisted. We could do nothing but watch as he relived Megan's last days, relived everything she'd stood for and done. Watch as two strong guys who looked like they could take anything, do anything, dissolved into tears, and seemed to lose height and weight before our eyes. We all turned in for the night soon afterwards. I lay there, staring at the ceiling, when there was a knock at the door to my dorm.

I opened it and Jack shuffled in and slumped at the end of my bed. He looked so small and so vulnerable that I instinctively wrapped my arms round him and we just sat there. He didn't try and kiss me or anything and I didn't want him to. Not because there were ten other girls (albeit sleeping) in the room. It wasn't about that. It was more like we'd taken all these different chaotic emotions we'd been going through these past days and blended them together to come up with a smoothie of pure friendship. Platonic plus. It must have been an hour or so before he even spoke, and when he did his voice was low and cracked.

'Thanks for being my friend, Noa. I know I've been pushing things lately, and I shouldn't have. I guess if you've wanted something for so long you just kind of keep chasing it. Like it becomes part of you. Even if you've moved past it. Even if your heart now lies elsewhere. Does that make any sense?'

I nodded. In its own messed-up way it made a lot of sense. Jack wasn't over Megan and I wasn't over Raf. We'd been trying this thing, this 'us', as it'd always been there in the background. An unspoken, unacted upon presence. Now we'd done it, we'd acted and somehow or other we'd banished the ghost in the process. We sat there in silence again although I knew Jack hadn't finished. Knew he had something else on his mind. Something else messing with his thoughts. Finally it spilled out.

'He didn't try to contact me, Noa. All these years, he let

me just go on thinking he was dead. How could someone do that? Just walk away from their son?'

I didn't get much sleep last night. I got stuck in a nightmare/wake-up/nightmare cycle and I kept returning to the same point I'd left off. Like I was watching a horror film while being trigger happy with the pause/play button on the remote. They weren't gory dreams. No one was being killed or chased or hurt or anything, but in a way that made it worse. I was in an ice cave, or rather a series of ice tunnels. The walls contained people and furniture and stuff from everyday life, but frozen into weird artificial positions – like they'd been ice-taxidermied. I was the only creature alive, moving. The first scene was of kids from school, no one I recognised, just random kids, sitting frozen at desks, while a teacher, no, an exam invigilator, stalked the back. I could handle that. The second I couldn't handle at all. There were three figures. Three girls standing still and pointing at me. I peered closer and made out their crystallised faces. Daisy, Megan and Ella, just standing there and pointing at me. Accusing me. I'd killed them. It was my fault. Befriend Noa and you die. I shut my eyes and hurried past and then wished I hadn't. Round the corner, in a cave, an ice scene of their own were Mum and Dad. They were sat on the brown sofa in our living room, holding a picture, a photo of me. Mum's face had aged by about ten years and Dad was thin and stooped. I tried yelling at them, telling them I was OK, that I was alive and they didn't need to worry anymore, but they couldn't hear me. Nothing I could say or do reached them. I screamed, but no sound came out. Instead shards of ice started shooting out of my windpipe and then burying their way backwards, choking me.

I woke, covered in a film of sweat, surrounded by the other girls in the dorm, finding Nell sat next to me, stroking my arm. Apparently I'd been calling out in my sleep. Woken everyone.

'Sorry,' I mumbled. But my thoughts were elsewhere. My thoughts were on Mum and Dad. I had to visit them. I had to tell them I was OK. Since we'd reached the First City, Raf, Jack and Lee had all independently warned me against trying to make contact. The Ministry would be watching them for sure and it was the quickest way to get caught.

'I get it, Noa,' Raf had said. 'I want to check on my mum too. Desperately so. But it's too risky right now. And you'd be endangering them too.'

I'd listened to him, nodding in all the right places, but I couldn't sit here and not at least try. They were my parents. A girl can't just walk away from her parents.

This morning, I dressed quickly, planning to leave straight away. I didn't want any questions so I hid in the bathroom while everyone was having breakfast. Ten minutes became twenty became thirty. It was quiet. Peering through the banisters, the stairs looked empty.

Now.

I went for it. But, I couldn't have timed it worse. Racing down the steps, two at a time, I collided with Jack's dad, flanked by Jack, Lee and Nell.

'Glad to see you're keen, Noa,' he said. 'I was worried you'd forgotten.'

My confusion must have shown as he continued, 'The tour? Remember?'

Of course, he'd mentioned it last night. He was going to give us the proper tour of the building, get us up to speed on their projects and then find out more about our plans to alter the uploads. There was no getting out of it. Finding my parents would have to wait till later.

'Where's Raf?' I asked Lee, suddenly conscious of his absence.

'Headache,' Lee replied. 'A bad one,' he added and then speeded up so that he was out of step with me. Whatever was going on, he clearly didn't want to talk about it.

I wasn't going to let him avoid me that easily. Grabbing his arm, I slowed him down and span him round.

'Lee, what aren't you telling me?'

'It's nothing, Noa.'

'We need to get him to a doctor. To a specialist.'

Lee didn't reply. His look was enough. And I knew he was right. We couldn't take him anywhere. We'd need a proper high-up brain consultant and the only access was through Ministry-approved channels. Channels obviously closed to us.

I rejoined the group, reluctantly at first, but soon became interested, drawn in. The Opposition headquarters are really quite something. Obviously, the basement torture cellars aren't anything to write home about, but the rest of the operation is staggering.

From the outside the building looks like any other in the street. As run down as you'd expect in this part of town. There was a shop front on the ground floor selling wholesale kitchen equipment, in keeping with the residential/business mix. The manager was a guy called Sam. He didn't know everything, but he knew enough. Enough to never go up or down the stairs. Enough to have a panic button under the sales desk to press in case of unwelcome visitors.

Next to the shop entrance were letterboxes and doorbells purporting to belong to flats on the floors above. All in the names of law-abiding, card-carrying citizens of the Territory.

'Loyal to us,' Jack's dad explained.

If anyone came investigating the front would obviously only hold up so long. And then they'd have to disappear and restart from scratch. They'd done it before, Jack's dad said almost proudly, and they'd do it again if need be.

At the top of the house sat the dorms, kitchen and rec room. I already knew that. Below them was where the real work was done. First we were shown a computer room, filled with terminals, monitors, servers and bundles of wire attached to lots of little black boxes that left me confused but Lee in ecstatic glee. I don't think I've ever seen a smile so wide. Like it was eating his face.

'For surveillance, and organising campaigns,' Jack's dad explained. 'If someone in the Ministry sneezes, we know about it,' he said smugly.

His smugness irritated me so I couldn't resist throwing in a, 'Well, why do Opposition members keep getting caught the whole time then?'

Jack's dad's smile remained in place but became a good few degrees colder. 'Sometimes we need to make calculated sacrifices,' he replied. God! So they gave certain people up. Let them go so the Ministry would think they had total control. This man was a robot.

The surveillance room was ruled by Mina, a really short woman in her late twenties with mousy-brown hair. The mouse comparison ended there. Everything else about her was big. Big personality. Big, bellowing laugh. Super loud yelling at Lee when he started to tap at a keyboard without permission. I liked her immediately.

'How did you get all this stuff?' I asked, incredulous. In the Territory, ordinary non-Ministry peeps couldn't even own a mobile phone let alone a den of super-spy computer stuff.

'We have our sources. People who support us,' Mina replied. I waited to hear more but Mina's mouth was a zipped pencil case, one where the zip's half broken off so it's locked shut permanently. In her mind we clearly weren't proper Opposition yet. Not to be trusted with secrets.

We were in there for a while as Jack's dad had to disappear and 'check on something'. Lee used this as an opportunity to ask Mina if she'd look over his code for the new upload. He showed her what he'd come up with at the Server and Mina decreed that it could potentially have worked but only contained about half the relevant data and was *inelegant*. For Mina, code was as much an art as a science. If we were going to hack Childes' brains, an idea she seemed immediately taken with, we were going to do it in an effective and *beautiful* way.

Jack's dad returned and the tour continued. Next to Surveillance sat Operations. As Jack's dad pushed open the door, I fully expected to see Milk Teeth (real name Jon: it doesn't suit him) in charge, pointing at a whiteboard with a stick that he was also using to beat people. But

Milk Teeth wasn't there. Simon was. A quieter, greyer Simon than I'd met yesterday but Simon nonetheless. There was a steely intelligence to his eyes and a determination in the set of his jaw that made me feel instantly safer – that we might actually stand a chance. It also helped that he was unrolling a series of blueprints of buildings and discussing possible entrances, exits and ventilation ducts with a group of five earnest assistants. Maybe he was already planning how to get into the Ministry to find the digital key we needed.

Before I had an opportunity to ask, we were swept out again, down a flight of stairs and into a smaller room on the first floor: Security. Milk Teeth's domain, which totally made sense and seemed to consist of him training minions in how to inflict massive amounts of pain. Everyone in there seemed to have muscles in inverse proportion to their IQ. Ironically, his room was the prettiest. The window looked out on to a flat roof, which was covered in plant pots – their vegetable garden. The leaves and flowers made Milk Teeth seem even creepier, like sweet musicbox tinkling when the evil clown appears in a horror film.

It was a relief to leave there and check out Rally Coordination – basically a box room run by Jasmine, an energetic older woman whose thin but wiry arms looked like they'd been born holding a placard. Her work was more sensitive and she had a network of informants, feeding back information as to whose sensibilities might be shifting and who might be persuaded into voicing their anger.

Finally, we reached the innocuous-sounding Planning where Jack's dad was based. It was home to serial-killer-style wall plans with red dots, photos of groups of people with one face circled, close-up images of buildings with numbers next to them: 351; 274; 54 and so on. It made my chest constrict.

'And these are…?' I asked quietly.

'Targets,' came Jack's dad's clipped reply. 'Viable targets that would deplete enemy resources.'

I swallowed. He said it so coldly. These were people, with families, buildings with workers. Targets, all of them. The Opposition I knew about didn't assassinate and bomb. Didn't kill. The Ministry often claimed they did as an excuse to go after their members and crush the rallies, but Dad had shown me the truth. Revealed the Ministry lies. But now they seemed to be changing strategy. Becoming more and more violent.

'Why now?' I asked quietly.

Jack's dad seemed pleased by my interest.

'We've been organising rallies and acts of minor sabotage for years and nothing's changed. More and more kids are being shipped off. The fact is placards achieve nothing. Words achieve nothing. The Ministry's been telling everyone that we kill people, that we're responsible for countless atrocities. That we've blown up Womb Pods, for God's sake. When they accused us of that, it changed things. It changed me. I thought it's about time we started living up to our reputation.'

There was something about the 'I' that made it jump out from the rest of the words with a different volume or resonance. He was clearly the driving force behind the new direction the Opposition was taking, and proud of it.

'But what about our upload-hacking plan?' I asked. 'We can influence people without killing anyone!'

'The practicality of that idea has yet to be determined. These are plans we've been working on for some time. You can't make an omelette without breaking eggs, Noa,' he added tritely, hailing from a generation where eggs came in shells from chickens, rather than as yellow, Mucor-based powder in a box.

But breaking eggs doesn't always result in an omelette, I thought. Sometimes you just end up with a smashed-up globular mess on the floor. I didn't say it, though, didn't say anything as my eyes were suddenly glued to a picture that seemed to leap out towards me, about a metre off the wall.

The Laboratory. The Laboratory was a target. Mum was a target.

A soft, 'No!' escaped my mouth. Jack's dad followed my gaze and then shot a look at me. There was no mistaking its meaning: *weakling*.

'You can't!' I said, louder this time.

'The Laboratory is a viable target, Noa.'

'But there're innocent people in there!' I continued, my voice rising to a shout. 'Innocent people you'll hurt, you'll kill!'

'We don't hurt innocent people,' Jack's dad retorted coldly. 'The people who work at the Laboratory, who *experiment* at the Laboratory, they're not innocent. In no way are they innocent, Noa. And your mother might well not even be there.'

'You're wrong and she would be there. Of course she'd be there…'

Jack's dad interrupted me. Crushed me with a glare and a raised hand.

'We must put the good of the cause before everything else. We must set other emotions aside. We need to start inflicting damage or we will never win.'

I could see Jack begin to ball his hand into a fist, recognising himself as an 'other emotion', something to be 'set aside'. I should have comforted him, but I couldn't stay there. Breathing the same air as that man. I ran towards the door.

'Noa,' Jack's dad shot at my back. 'Don't even think about trying to warn anyone. That would make you a traitor and we don't look kindly on traitors.'

I reached the entrance to my dorm, but didn't enter. I went past and into the boys' dorm instead. Raf was asleep, but I shook him awake.

'They want to kill my mum,' I sobbed at him. 'They're going to kill my mum!'

I left before dawn. I had it all planned out. The whole communal living, no fixed breakfast time, and lots of individual projects thing meant that no one should miss me as long as I was back by nine. The only other person up in the dorm was Nell, but I don't think she even registered my presence – she was just sitting there, lost in thought, staring strangely intently at a Mucor packet.

I was on the landing when I bumped into Raf. His eyes were red-rimmed and his skin was pale, but at least he was out of bed, standing. He didn't seem surprised to see me. More like he'd been waiting for me.

'Don't try and talk me out of it,' I whispered. 'You know I have to do this.'

'I know. I was going to say be careful.'

'Cover for me, OK?'

'OK… But you can't go out the front door. There're people in the shop already. I went to check.'

I raised an eyebrow.

'I know you, Noa. I didn't want you to get caught.'

I thought for a moment.

'I'll use the flat roof… But I'll need you to shut the window behind me. Can you do that?'

Raf laughed. A quiet, mocking laugh. 'I know I'm a

pretty weak loser at the moment, but I think I can handle a window!'

'Sorry,' I replied, smiling. Smiling as his eyes managed a tiny sparkle, as his teeth headed in the direction of wolf.

We crept down the two flights of stairs to Security, listened at the door – silence – and ducked inside. Raf held open the sash window while I ducked through and climbed out on to the roof.

Three deep breaths and then I lowered myself over the side, dangling like someone stuck on the monkey bars at the playground. My arms felt like they were being wrenched out of their sockets and shook from strain. God – the pavement seemed a long way away. My head swam but there was no turning back now. Also, from a practical point of view, I've never managed a pull up so I couldn't exactly lift myself up on to the roof again. The only way was down. 'Good luck,' Raf mouthed as I let go, dropping to the pavement below. My legs shuddered as they absorbed the impact.

I'd done it. I was out on the streets. The emphasis now was on blending in, on not being stopped. I wasn't a total denser, I'd prepared for this. I was wearing indistinctive, blend-in clothes and had a cap tightly pulled down over my face. From across the street or from a 45-degree-angled camera, you probably couldn't even tell if I was a boy or a girl. Walking briskly, but not too fast, nothing to attract attention, I covered the streets to the other side of town, to our apartment block. My parents' block. After what I'd done, what I'd put them through, I guess I'd given up any claim to call it home.

Passing the corner of 23rd and 7th Street I could make out an Opposition rally ahead. Jasmine's work, no doubt. The slogans were unchanged: *Stop Killing our Kids; Space for All; Ministry Murderers*, but there seemed to be more energy to it. The chants were louder. More defiant. It'd be the next set of parents. The ones with kids facing exams in nine months' time. The ones with people to lose. I wanted to get closer, talk to someone, but I knew I couldn't risk it. Already police sirens wailed their approach as they came to break it up. This was the last place in the world I should be right now. Ducking down a side street, I worked my way across the City, pausing every now and then as I got my bearings, an explorer of old navigating by buildings and landmarks instead of stars.

My heart triple-jumped inside my chest as the apartment block finally came into view. After everything that I'd been through these last months, I'd sort of expected it to look different. To have changed like I had. But apart from the fact the leaves were now falling from the trees outside, it was the same. Right down to the policeman loitering on the front steps.

Marcus.

Damn.

He'd recognise me, be sure to.

How to distract him?

I contemplated breaking a window of the neighbouring block I now crouched behind in order to set off an alarm and draw him away. But the rational section of my brain knew this was the densest idea. There were so many ways it could go wrong. I had to wait. There was nothing else for it. Wait for my chance.

My legs were stiff, rusted into squatting position by the time Marcus finally left the steps and continued on his beat. Forcing them into action, I was off, hobble-running up the steps and to the front door as the blood gradually returned to my feet.

5 – 4 – 8 – 2

With shaking fingers, I punched the numbers into the keypad and the door opened with a click. Thank God the building supervisor hadn't changed the code.

My head resolutely down, eyes focused on feet, I climbed the three flights of stairs to the flat. In my head I rehearsed what I'd say. *Mum, Dad – I'm so sorry for leaving like that... I missed you so much... Mum – you're in danger.* Tears were free flowing down my cheeks. Who would open the door? Dad? Mum? It was just before seven-thirty so neither of them should have left for work yet unless there'd been some kind of emergency.

I stood in front of the door to Flat 8 and took a deep breath to calm my nerves. I'd never before thought how eight looks like a rotated infinity sign. Infinite love from flat number eight. Home. I was home at last. Then I balled my hand into a fist, raised it and knocked. Twice. Rap rap. That's how people in my family knock. You get some rap-de-rappers out there, but we were rap-rap people. Always would be.

The door started to open and my mouth widened in unison, like the hinge was surgically attached to my lips.

'Hello?'

An unfamiliar voice, female but low and soft. My brain short-circuited. Who was this person?

'Sorry, can I help you?'

The voice again. The person. There was a youngish woman with blue glasses and orange lipstick in my parents' flat.

'I'm looking for Mr and Mrs Blake,' I said, acid edging its way up my oesophagus, burning.

'Um. I think you've got the wrong flat, love. Colin…' she shouted to the back, 'you don't know a Mr and Mrs Blake, do you?'

'No, don't think so,' came the muffled reply.

I angled my head so I could see further through the door. The sofa was wrong. It was green. Our sofa was brown. Why wasn't the sofa brown? And why was there a standard lamp? And where was our blue-and-white checked rug? There's supposed to be a blue-and-white checked rug in the hall!

My chest tightened and I couldn't breathe. My knees

started to buckle as the squeezing intensified and my brain lost oxygen. I grabbed at the doorframe for support. As my fingers closed round the wood they touched something else. Thinner, lighter. I pulled it out and found myself staring at the torn remains of a piece of yellow paper.

My parents' flat had been repossessed.

The Ministry had them.

'Can I get you something, a glass of water, perhaps?' The woman was talking to me, but her voice seemed far away, like it was coming from a distant speaker system.

Ignoring her, I stumbled towards the stairs. I had to get back. I had to get back to the others.

It was raining when I left the building. Large drops that landed with a splash and soaked through your clothes and obscured your vision. That mingled with tears and flowed salty sweet into your mouth.

I wasn't looking where I was going. I wasn't concentrating. I forgot that I wasn't supposed to run and sprinted down a side alley. I was shaking all over and then, slowly, ever so slowly, my muscles stilled. Something primeval took me over. Something dark and animal, thousands of years old. Something that raised my head to the clouds, daring the rain to pummel my face. Something that let out a howl of despair and a declaration of war.

Arriving back outside the Opposition headquarters building, I started to head for the side alley and then stopped. This wasn't a crawl in through a roof-terrace window moment. After what had happened, I didn't care who saw me. Flinging open the door to the shop, I stormed straight down the stainless steel pans and sieves aisle and through the door marked 'staff only'. Then I was off, pounding up the stairs, a trail of wet footprints and reverberating treads in my wake. Lee poked his head over the banisters and couldn't conceal his shock at my appearance. Wet, wild-eyed, radiating rage.

'Noa…' he began tentatively, 'everyone's looking for you.'

'Where is he?' I demanded.

'Who?'

'Jack's dad. Where is he?'

'In the rec room. What's going on, Noa?'

I didn't answer him but instead pushed past and kept on going. The door to the rec room was already open. There were about twenty people sitting around, talking, finishing their breakfast. Everyone fell silent as I appeared in the doorway, the murmur of the TV on the far wall the only sound.

'Seize her,' Jack's dad's sharp order. Two girls approached and grabbed my arms.

'Let go of me,' I spat. 'Take your hands off me, now!' They ignored me and just dug their fingers in harder.

'You disobeyed orders,' Jack's dad barked. 'You went to warn her. I told you we don't tolerate traitors.'

'I didn't tell anyone!' I yelled back. 'There was no one there to tell. And you KNEW that, didn't you? That's why you said she might not be at work, isn't it? 'Cos you KNEW they'd taken her. You listen into and watch what they do and you KNEW. How could you know that and not tell me?'

'Take her downstairs,' Jack's dad ordered, ignoring me. 'NO!'

Not my voice, but Jack's. He'd positioned himself behind me, blocking the doorway.

'No one is taking her anywhere. Is it true, Dad? Did you know?' Jack stared at his dad. Daring him to lie. Daring him to break the thread of trust that was starting to bind them. Jack's dad blinked first.

'I knew,' he replied, quietly. His voice less certain now, seeking understanding. 'But revealing that information wouldn't have been helpful to the cause. Noa was more likely to leave, to get distracted, to expose us.'

'Because the cause is everything, isn't it?' Jack shot back. 'God forbid anyone should value anything else!' Jack's dad flinched as the words assaulted him.

The girls made to move me again, but still Jack blocked the doorway.

'You touch her and you lose me forever,' Jack shouted. 'It'll be me that walks away this time and never looks back. Me.'

There was a horrid, solid silence while we waited. And the thing is, it was like I wasn't even there, like I was just observing it. I didn't really care what they did to me, how they hurt me. No one could hurt me as much as that piece of yellow paper had done.

'Let her go,' Jack's dad had backed down. Jack put his arms towards me to hug me when suddenly everyone froze.

'Noa!' Lee's voice this time, from the far corner. 'Noa, what have you done?'

I turned and followed twenty-odd pairs of eyes to the television screen. Lee had turned up the volume so we all could hear. Not that it was the sound that hit me first. It was the image. A photo of me, my face raised to the sky, screaming and next to it the image from my old Citizen's ID card. The word 'WANTED' stamped across the top of the screen. The Ministry knew I was in the First City. I was an idiot. I'd broken the first rule. The only rule of remaining undercover.

I'd looked up.

I must have gone into a kind of trance or passed out or something as next thing I knew, I was back in my bed, Raf perched on the end, watching over me like some kind of stone angel at a tomb.

'So?' I said, bleakly. What else was there to say? 'I don't suppose I imagined that then?'

'Nope,' came Raf's reply. He'd tried to make it sound jokey, but it fell flat. A pancake collapsing in on itself mid-flip.

'I'm such a denser,' I mumbled.

'You were upset. Anyone would have lost control.'

'You wouldn't.'

'You don't know that, Noa.'

'So, I guess I'm not going to be allowed out any time soon.'

'No … I guess not. There's a reward … a reward for handing you in.'

'How much?' It was always money. The number of zeros corresponding to the importance of the fugitive. I wondered how much I was worth. A thousand? Ten thousand?

'It's not money.' Raf swallowed and something about the way his Adam's apple bobbed up and down told it was going to be bad. Really bad.

'It's a free pass for your kid into the Territory.'

The words lodged in my throat and choked me. This was another level. Anyone would betray me for that. The guaranteed protection of your child, the ability to skip the TAA. It was the sort of thing people would kill for. Rational, normal people. My mum had arguably done worse. There were no two ways about it; I was screwed.

I stuffed my pillow over my head to muffle my scream and then emerged again, red-eyed.

'Why?' I asked. 'Why do they want me that much?'

'Because I think they've worked out that we did the impossible. We broke out and back in again. I expect they want to know how.'

'Great!' I laughed bitterly. 'So these past few months have been for what exactly! We're still nowhere near getting the key for the uploads. We've hooked up with an Opposition who just seem to want to blow everything up. We've done nothing. Achieved nothing, except KILL MY PARENTS!'

A flash of something crossed Raf's brow.

'What is it?' I demanded.

'Nothing,' he replied. But he was fobbing me off. I know him too well. His left eye squints a bit when he's lying.

'Tell me.'

'They're not dead. After the pictures of you and the promise of a reward they showed images of your mum and dad.'

I wanted to believe. I wanted to believe so much.

'Pictures prove nothing. They could have been from weeks ago.'

'Not pictures, video, with them confirming today's date. They're alive, Noa.'

'Oh thank God! Thank God!' It was almost too much, a straw to clutch at. They were prisoners but still alive. There was still some hope that I could save them somehow. I leapt off the bed and started to jig around with manic energy. I hadn't killed my parents!

I tried to pull Raf up to join me but he resisted and pulled me back down next to him.

'Noa… Oh God, this is hard… I'm going to tell you because if I don't someone else will. This is a trap, you have to realise this. It's clearly a Ministry trap.'

'Just tell me.'

'They said that if you hand yourself in, your parents are free to go.'

'I'm handing myself in.'

I spoke as loudly and forcefully as I could and my voice filled the rec room, making everyone look up from their dinner. I'd thought about it all afternoon. How could I do anything else?

'NO!' a simultaneous command from Raf and Jack, echoed around the room by additional voices.

'Don't be stupid, Noa…' Jack started to try and reason with me when his dad cut him off and stalked over to me, bristling with anger.

'Come with me,' he snapped, dragging me into the kitchen. This time Jack let him take me. He probably wasn't going to torture and dispose of me in the kitchen. There was only so much damage he could manage with a blunt cutlery set. Jack's dad shut the door. This conversation was clearly for us, not for show, and when he began to speak his voice was quieter, with an edge of desperation rather than fury.

'There's going to be no debate this time. You are not doing this, Noa. What do you seriously think is going to happen if you just march up to Ministry HQ and turn yourself in? That they'll let your parents go, with a pat on the back and a full ration card?'

The yellow flecks in his eyes were fireballs. I looked at the floor.

'I have to try,' I murmured. 'They're there because of me. I can't just sit here and do nothing!'

'They won't let them go, Noa. You know that. They'll still kill them. And they'll kill you. But not before they've made you tell them everything you know about us.'

'I won't talk.'

'They'll make you. You won't be able to help yourself.

You'll betray us all. Raf, Nell, Lee ... Jack – they'll end up dead or tortured in some Ministry basement. Because of you. And the rest of us – Mina, Jasmine, Simon – think of them? You're not the only one with family. We've all got responsibilities – people depending on us. Jon's got kids, Mina too. Do you want them waking up tomorrow knowing one of their parents has been taken? You might not think I care about anyone or anything other than the cause. That's not true. I do care. I thought about Jack every day I was away. I just couldn't see him. I couldn't put him in danger. It was safer for him this way.'

If I didn't know better I'd have thought tears were forming in the corner of his eyes.

'So, Noa. I wish I could get rid of you or lock you up, but I can't. Jack won't let me. So instead, I'm asking you. I'm begging you. Please don't do this. If not for me for Jack. Think about Jack.'

With that, he strode out the kitchen and I was left to myself and my thoughts.

Family.

How messed up is family. You do the best and the worst things to protect the ones you love. Blood and genes, the sun around which we all orbit. I thought of Jack and his dad. Jack's horrific mum. Raf's ... oh God. Oh God. I just realised. If the Ministry had taken my parents, they'd have taken Raf's, too. He must realise this. He must be going through exactly what I'm going through, I'd just been too selfish to see it.

I hurried out the kitchen to find him.

He was sat in the corner, nose in a book.

'I'm sorry,' I blurted out. 'I didn't think about your mum too. I'm so sorry.'

He wrapped his arms round me and kissed the top of my forehead.

I didn't need to explain what I was talking about and he didn't need to respond. We understood each other and that was enough. As close to telepathy as we were ever going to get.

The night seemed to stretch out forever. I couldn't sleep, the conversation with Jack's dad on repeat in my head. I gave up trying at about four and went downstairs instead. I got a glass of water and let myself out of the window to the roof garden. I know I wasn't supposed to leave the building, but there weren't any cameras here and I was still technically on the building even if I wasn't inside. The growing plants were somehow comforting. Life. Renewal.

A couple of hours later, dawn was finally breaking. I heard the window squeak and to my surprise Mina crawled out and sat down. When she saw me, she practically jumped out of her skin.

'Sorry. I wasn't expecting anyone,' she giggled. 'This is my sort of morning ritual, before everyone's up. I come here to phone my boys.' She waved her mobile. Totally illegal, unlicensed. Perk of the job. 'They're early risers,' she continued, 'it's my boost for the day. Beats caffeine, though you're probably too young to remember that.'

She was wrong. I remember the smell of coffee in the kitchen. Mum cradling the mug like a second baby.

'Have I shown you photos of them?'

I shook my head. She eagerly reached into her pocket and brought out two pictures. Sami and Guv. Four and six. Jet-black hair, light brown skin, snub nosed with cherub cheeks. Mina's love for them shone from her every gesture, her every syllable.

'They're with their dad. It'd be too dangerous here for them. I get to see them once a week. We arrange something so it's safe. It'll be different soon ... sometime. For now it's better this way. I'd do anything to protect them, you know that? *Anything*.' Mina was speaking to the photos now, to her boys rather than to me, and her voice cracked with emotion. I think she even forgot I was there for a minute, she was so lost in her own thoughts and dreams, her own responsibilities. I felt like an intruder.

'I'll give you some space.'

I'm not sure if Mina heard me or not, but I stood up

and let myself back in through the window. I'd meant to close the window and head straight up to my room, or to the rec room at least, but instead I stayed, sat on the floor, next to the open window. The only explanation I can think is that I wanted to hear a mum's voice. A mum talking to her kids. A mum making her kids feel safe.

Mina had her back to me so some of her words were lost or muffled. I could hear most of them though. It was clear that it was Mina's husband who answered the phone. There was a tenderness to Mina's voice, no forced joviality. A mask dropped. But then tenderness was replaced by tension and Mina's tone sharpened.

'No. No … I know about the place. I don't know if it's one place or two? Maybe one place but we have two kids remember.'

What were they talking about? Then it clicked. The reward. The reward for handing me in. *A place for your kid in the Territory.* The bottom of my stomach fell away and I could hear the rush of blood in my ears. Why was I surprised? I shouldn't blame her. Him. It was natural. Natural to put your kids first. I had to go though. Get out of here. Now.

I sprang up to standing, my elbow banging against the window. Mina turned round at the noise and our eyes met. Locked.

I made to leave, but her voice dragged me back.

'Noa, wait. Please, wait.'

'There's no time,' I said quietly. 'They're coming, aren't they?'

Her eyes shifted gear.

'No! God, no, Noa! Mark, my husband, he was just ranting. He'd never. I'd never.'

'It's OK,' I replied. 'I understand. I really do.'

She paused and her eyes deepened into brown pools that radiated sincerity. 'I was tempted for a minute, I admit it, but you're part of us now and that means you're family. Family in the way that counts. And you never hurt family.'

I found Jack's dad in his office. He was sat at his desk talking to Jasmine but on seeing me standing in the doorway, he asked her to leave, to 'give us a minute'.

'Well?' He didn't bother to stand up.

I closed the door before replying. Then went over and sat across from him. We were going to discuss this as equals; I wasn't going to stand and squirm.

'I'm not going to hand myself in.'

The tension visibly fell from his shoulders.

'Good decis...'

'I'm not finished yet. There's a condition. I won't hand myself in if you give the upload plan a chance. Delay the bombing. Just for a week. Give it a week and if it doesn't work out you can go back to blowing everything up. You can even blame any bombs on me. Make me the scapegoat, they want me anyway. I'll walk into the Ministry building, hand myself in and confess to it all. Just give this a chance first.'

Jack's dad looked at me. Grey eyes serious. Weighing things up.

'You really think this could work?'

I met his eyes, returned his stare.

'I do. We need to find the digital key, but as soon as we have that, it could work. We have to try. It would undermine the Ministry in a way that bombs and bloodshed never could. Think about it – the Childes, their most ardent supporters, realising that they've been brainwashed and rising up against their creators? Rebelling against the TAA. The system would lose all its support. It would crumble.'

A beat.

'I understand if you need time to think it over.'

'I don't.' The reply came quicker than I'd expected. 'You have a week. You'll have all our resources at your disposal for a week.'

'Thank you!' I gushed, all composure gone. 'Thank you so, so much.'

'After that, you do everything we say.'

Jack's dad stood up and I kind of hovered uncomfortably, not sure what was expected of me now.

'Well,' he said, raising an eyebrow. 'Don't you have some work to do?'

The atmosphere's changed. Got more serious. You can tell by the fact that no one speaks at lunch, other than *pass the bread, grunt, water anyone? Grunt.*

Since Jack's dad gave the go-ahead, all the focus has been on getting hold of the digital key. We were embarking on a three-pronged mission. Simon was leading a team doing close-up reconnaissance of the Ministry headquarters, checking out a potential way in through a side ventilation duct that they'd identified from the blueprints. Jasmine was orchestrating the biggest rally for some time, using it as bait to lure police officers away from the Ministry building, towards Milk Teeth's gang who would attack them to weaken their defences.

And what was I doing? I was staying put at the Opposition headquarters. Nominally to help Mina and provide 'administrative back-up', but really so I didn't flash my face at any more security cameras or go back on my promise to Jack's dad not to hand myself in. Raf was here too. Still weak, he wasn't in a position to be sprinting away from any security guards or police. Also, as he was linked to me 'cos we disappeared at the same time from the same place, everyone would be looking for him, too. I'd turned him into another liability. Lee made him swear he'd rest. Nothing more.

I enjoyed helping Mina, though. Still wary of dislodging a lead or accidentally hitting a button of fundamental importance, I tiptoed round her as she worked, handing her the occasional sheet of paper, reading out characters from a screen when directed to do so.

'What's the idea behind all the rallies?' I asked as we stopped for a mid-morning 'biscuit' break. Parsnip thins. As close to a biscuit as, well, as a parsnip can be. Which is basically light years. 'They're always broken up by the police and just end up with people getting arrested and worse.'

'They're the only way we have of communicating with ordinary people. Getting our message out there. The News, what's called news anyway, is Ministry lies, all of it. Our only chance of changing things is to tell people what's really going on. And…' Mina paused to reach for another slice of dried-up parsnip '…the rallies let people know that they're not alone in their feelings. That there are others who want to resist. Who want to change things. All we need is to keep pushing until we hit a critical mass. A tipping point. Then it will all crumble.'

'And what then?' I asked. This is what me and Raf had never been able to pin down. Like it or not, it was true: limited space meant limited numbers. It had to, to some extent, so you were still left with the question – who gets a space?

'I'm not sure, Noa. That's the truth of it. But there's got to be something better than this. Some system which isn't determined solely by money. The philosophy side isn't really my forte,' Mina continued with a laugh. 'I'm the computer geek!'

We ate in friendly silence for a few minutes, before the next question popped into my head.

'So, will it be in a safe or something?' I asked.

'Will what?' Mina replied, mid-bite.

'The code. The private digital-signature thingy we need to send out an upload?'

Mina burst out laughing, spraying a cloud of parsnip crumbs over the floor in the process.

'You really know nothing about computers, do you?'

'Nothing,' I replied sheepishly.

In my head, the signature was written down on a piece of paper, maybe one of those formal scrolls with a wax seal, and sat in a gold box behind a coded door, to be taken out and copied when needed. My head is a denser that has watched too many heist movies.

Mina tried to explain, her tone verging into *patronise a moron* territory, but I guess I deserved it.

'My hope is that the Ministry uses the same private digital signature for all of its important communications. By infiltrating the headquarters, we hope to be able to access one such communication and determine the code from it.'

'So it wouldn't even need to be an upload then?'

'No, exactly. It could be something like a communication between army bases or a message from the Ministry of Education to a Waiting Place or from the Ministry of Science to a satellite.'

A satellite.

A shooting star of an idea arced its way across my mind.

'Don't go anywhere,' I said unnecessarily and bounced out the room, springs for legs, like a kid who'd just passed the TAA. As I sprinted to Lee's dorm and rummaged through the storage cupboard my whole body was a mosquito swarm of excitement. Ehehehehheheh, the cells buzzed.

I found his backpack at the bottom of the pile. Bashed up, ripped in places, one of the handles literally hanging on by a thread. I thrust my hand inside and it touched something cold and metallic. It was still there.

BANG! I flung open the door to Surveillance a little too hard on my return and the door knob crashed into the wall.

'Noa? What's got into you? Mina looked amused. But amused on the edge of teetering into pretty mad.

'Sorry. Sorry. But look. Look Mina! Will this do?'

'What is it?'

'Part of a satellite.'

Mina's excitement was such that her hands literally trembled as she held the satellite part. For a moment I thought she might drop it and it'd smash to pieces on the floor, our hopes ending with a fumble.

But she didn't – drop it that is – she got herself together and turned it over, examining it from all angles, using tweezers to untangle wires and identify their source. Like a palaeontologist studying a fossil to determine the creature it once was.

'Can we use it?' I asked, my voice strained and husky.

'It's rusted in parts. There's corrosion here, here and here, but … but we might still be able to retrieve some data. There's only one way to find out! I'm going to need you to stay silent so I can focus.'

I nodded and sat there in mute awe as Mina delved into boxes, pulling out wires, clips, circuit boards, connectors and started connecting everything up to a terminal. She tapped at a keyboard, entering fragments of code, commands, her forehead creasing and unfolding, a slow-motion earthquake as she digested the information being fed back to her.

I couldn't keep quiet any longer.

'So, it is working? Can you get the signature?'

Three slow beats.

'Yes, Noa. Yes, I think I can.'

The others returned late afternoon, their arrival announced by the heavy trudge of boots up the stairs.

We swept out of Surveillance to meet them, our massive grins semi-neutralised by a swathe of glum faces. I caught Jack's eye and raised an eyebrow.

'It's off,' he said glumly. 'Mission's off. The building's impenetrable. Even the side duct is alarmed. We're back to the bombs. I'm sorry, Noa. You know we tried. We gave it everything.'

I mirrored his frown for a second and then my grin popped up again. Like a rubber duck you submerge in the bath that keeps coming back to the surface.

'Noa, don't you get it?!' Lee this time. 'This is bad news. Properly bad. Everything, the uploads, all our plans, it's over!'

'No, Lee' I replied. 'The thing is, it's really not!'

Raf emerged and joined us as my explanation was in full swing. He caught up quickly though. When I'd finished and everyone had been infected with our excitement, he snuck up behind me and kind of hovered for a moment before pinching my arm. I'm pretty sure the hesitation was him planning to hug me and then thinking better of it and going with this weird, semi-painful pinch instead.

'Sorry, don't know what that was,' he said, clearly slightly embarrassed, 'but good job, Noa. Always knew you weren't a total denser.' And then he flashed me one of his smiles. A proper wolf grin. Accompanied by green and blue 24-carat jewels. And my heart pinged.

'You've got the best moves, Raf Ferris,' I replied.

'Shut up, or I'll pinch you again,' he laughed and he ran round the room after me, pinching the air like a completely malc crab impersonator.

'Quiet!' Jack's dad shouted. 'We need to plan!'

As the room came to order, Lee marched over and hissed at me. 'Raf needs to rest at the moment. Not run around a room!'

'Sorry!' I hissed back, but not feeling remotely sorry, not for a minute. For a moment there, I had the real Raf back. The one that made my stomach flip and my heart soar.

The sun had set and the sky was a pure midnight blue, floodlit by a full moon. Everyone was sitting on the floor, in a circle. We looked like the meeting of an amateur magical society. To be fair we felt a little bit magic too. Mina had got the key. Lee had helped, a far more useful sidekick than I'd been. It hadn't taken them long in the end. A separate piece of code at the end of the satellite data.

'Very elegant,' was how she'd described it, admiringly. 'Very elegant indeed.'

Our plan was coming together, the stars were aligning.

'The issue under discussion,' Jack's dad began formally, 'is how best to break into the Server to send out the upload now that security will be greatly enhanced.'

'The army's involved,' Lee weighed in. 'We passed a squadron on our way here. So we'll probably have to get through some sort of blockade.'

Suggestions were flung around the room, all of which involved massive amounts of weapons and lots of 'collateral loss' as in people dying. Random soldiers. Our friends. My euphoria evaporated. More deaths. I couldn't handle more deaths.

Just as I thought I'd explode if I heard the word 'gun' one more time, Raf cut in.

'Do we have to go back to the Server at all?'

If you could read looks, then you'd have seen twenty-odd thought bubbles of *What? You denser!* shooting across the room towards him.

'What I mean is,' Raf continued, unabashed, 'Mina and Lee can code the upload here. We've got the digital key. All we'd be returning for is the antenna. The mast to broadcast it from. Wouldn't it be easier to build our own mast here?'

Everyone's eyes swivelled to Mina. Only she knew the mysteries of all things technical. Only she could translate the hieroglyphics.

'The boy's a genius!' she proclaimed, racing round the circle to pat Raf on the head. For a second it looked like she was initiating a game of Duck Duck Goose.

Thought bubbles morphed into grudging looks of respect and I leaned over and whispered in Raf's ear.

'Not a total denser after all.'

It's been decided. We're adopting Raf's plan. We've given ourselves a few days to build the mast and for Mina and Lee to make final adjustments to the upload.

Jack's dad wanted to put in coding to the effect that the Childes must all now rise up against the Ministry.

'You can't!' I'd cried. 'It'd make us just as bad as the Ministry. We've got to free them from mind control, not expose them to another version of it!'

Jack's dad looked unconvinced but, to my surprise, Jack joined in on my side.

'She's right, Dad,' he said. 'Trust me, I know they seem horrific. Freakoids. But they're still people. And we have to give them back their free will. We need to give them the truth and trust that they draw the right conclusions. And then act on them.'

'Thank you,' I whispered to Jack afterwards.

'It's nothing, Noa,' he replied with a half-smile. 'You

know me and Raf are never going to be best buds or anything, but he's a person. Not a lab rat. And I guess the other Childes are too.'

The fact that he said Childe not freakoid, and that it took me a few seconds to even realise this, showed how much we were all changing. How much people could change. And I felt this sense of calm optimism wrap itself around me like a dressing gown after a warm shower.

On the chosen day, the upload will go out at 4.30 p.m.

This means it will reach the Childes' Scribes when they're back from school to do 'homework'. Mina will work out the right frequency. It'll be sitting there, indistinguishable from other uploads. It wasn't uncommon for there to be two or even three uploads one day. There was no reason anyone should suspect anything.

We're nearly ready. Ready to change the world.

Never trust it. That feeling that everything's coming together and you're going to live happily ever after. If there's a God he's a cruel one. One that delights in toying with human emotions. Raising and dashing hopes like they're tiny fragile ornaments on a mantelpiece.

The warning system was triggered at 5 p.m. Most people were out hunting for scrap metal for the aerial.

Mina, Lee, Raf and me were working on the upload. Milk Teeth – I still can't call him Jon, it just feels wrong – was sleeping off a night-time mission. I don't know what it was but he still had dried blood above his left eyebrow.

Mina was in the middle of adjusting a string of code when she froze. And pointed. A small red light in the corner of the room was flashing on and off, on and off, a silent siren.

'No. NO! They're here. Oh God! They're here. Think. THINK!'

'What? Who?'

Without stopping to explain, Mina ran to wake Milk Teeth then herded us all into the rec room, turning on the TV.

'Channel Seven,' barked Milk Teeth.

'I know it's Seven,' Mina snapped back, nerves frayed. 'I've been here as long as you.'

Grainy video footage from the shop floor appeared on the screen. Two policemen stood in front of the sales' desk, a poster in their hands. A poster with my face on it.

'Sam must have pressed the alarm,' Mina said, her words coming out in a rush, running into each other. 'What do we do?'

'Bolthole. Now.' Milk Teeth took charge and sprang into action. 'Follow me.' He marched us into Jack's dad's office and up to a full-height bookcase. Standing to the left of it, he applied all his force and pushed. The bookcase slid to the right exposing a secret room. Windowless, airless, the size of a cupboard.

'Get in,' he instructed. 'Now.'

'What about you?' I asked.

'I can take care of myself.'

Once the three of us were inside, Milk Teeth pushed the bookcase back into position. We heard footsteps as he left the room and then silence.

It's horrible waiting in the dark. Your eyes dance around trying to make out features, patterns, anything, and your ears strain till they start popping. All you can hear is breathing. Your breathing. The breathing of the people next to you. In out, in out. Accelerating. Faster and faster even though you know you need to conserve oxygen. You can't run out – you don't know how long you're going to be there for. It wasn't long before we heard raised voices and boots on the stairs.

'You can't go up there!' Sam's voice. Yelling, projecting annoyance, but warning us as much as anything. Warning us that they were coming.

'That's private property. Of registered citizens. You have no right!'

'Our orders are to search every building. If they're registered, if they're not hiding anything, they've got nothing to worry about.'

Silence again perforated by scrapes, footsteps, muffled voices. The policemen were going through the whole building. They were going to find everything! The voices were coming closer. Creak. The door to the office was opening. The sound of files being rifled through, things being thrown around.

A different voice, deeper than before. 'What do you think? This stinks of Opposition to me.'

'I agree.'

Another pair of footsteps, quieter than before.

'Should we radio it in or keep trawling? Up the glory?'

'Maybe radio…'

Creak. A shout. Loud footsteps and then a crack and a scream. Thud, a heavy object hitting the floor. A second crack and a scream. And thud again.

When Milk Teeth pushed back the bookcase his whole face and body were covered in a dusting of red.

We didn't look at the bodies as we walked out of the room.

Jack's dad face went from stony grey to purple and back to grey again as Milk Teeth filled him in.

'But you're sure they didn't radio in?'

'I'm sure. I got to them first.'

'OK. OK. They won't know where they were immediately. We have time, limited time. Twenty-four hours. Maybe thirty-six.'

'What about cameras? CCTV?' I asked, my voice shaking despite my efforts to control it. 'Won't they be able to track the policemen to our building?'

'There aren't any cameras for a couple of blocks,' Mina replied. 'It's a rough area and we pay local kids to take them out. The policemen won't be missed till tomorrow. Even then it'll take them time to work out what happened.'

'I'll organise a distraction the other side of town,' Milk Teeth suggested. 'Draw attention away from here.'

'Good thinking,' said Jack's dad. 'Right, everyone, timetable's changed. Everything's moving forwards. The upload goes out tomorrow. Then we have to be out of here. Strip the place. Move on.'

He turned his attention to Mina. 'Is it doable?'

She nodded back. Already tired and traumatised by our time in the bolthole, but with a flinty look in her eye. 'We'll make it work.'

'What if they come before four-thirty?' Raf asked, quietly.

'We have ammunition, weapons,' Jack's dad replied. We can hold them off for a few hours. We'll make sure the upload goes out. Whatever it takes.'

The night was a blur of activity. Milk Teeth and Jack's dad were planning a distraction to the south of the city for first thing in the morning, eventually going for a car-park bomb. Loud explosion, lots of damage but no loss of life. That should keep the police well away from our building for most of the day. Jack was part of Simon's team, busy assembling the mast. Hammering and welding the metal pieces into position before crowning it with a satellite dish for transmission, ready to be lifted out on to the roof at the last minute. Nell was officially helping them, too, but was more of a bringer of water and snacks than anything.

Me and Raf were with Mina and Lee as they refined the upload, although I admit I fell asleep in my chair just before dawn. I woke as a dishevelled, dark-eye-bagged Mina announced its completion.

It starts with some facts about advanced Chemistry to hopefully normalise the experience for the Childes but then breaks into information about how the Ministry has been brainwashing them through the uploads, about how Norms are their equals rather than their inferiors.

We all regrouped in the rec room for breakfast. Milk Teeth was back, mission accomplished – over twenty cars now part of a massive bonfire that had to be contained.

'We have just one shot at this,' Jack's dad said. 'Have we covered every base?'

'Well, ideally we'd have tested the upload on a Childe, but obviously we can't,' Mina replied, wistfully.

I swallowed. Did they know about Raf? His hair had grown so long it covered the base of his neck, obscured the Node. I certainly hadn't mentioned it after the near-lynching Raf'd got at the Fort for being a freakoid. Maybe no one else had said anything either.

There was a pause that seemed to drag and stretch and bend.

Then it was broken by a voice.

Raf's.

'You can test it,' he said, quietly but clearly. 'You can test it on me.'

The silence that followed showed that no one had known. It was a buzzing silence, angry, hostile – a predator had infiltrated their hive.

Raf once more had to explain his background, his choice not to upload, as the mob transitioned through anger to doubt to admiration. I didn't listen to the words. My ears weren't working. It was like all the blood in my body had been diverted to my brain, which was about to explode.

Don't do it! I wanted to scream. *If you're too weak to be running around, you're far too weak to be sticking some lead in your head. To be messing with your brain. And what if*

Mina isn't as great as everyone says she is? She might be the best they've got but sometimes the best is still rubbish. Daisy's surgeon was supposed to be the best, wasn't he? What if it all goes wrong and you're not Raf anymore? What if it changes you and I lose you all over again but this time it's for good? What then?

Lee spoke first. 'This isn't a good idea, Raf. You're too weak.'

But Raf wasn't listening to him. He was looking at me. Really looking, concentrating like he was reading all the thoughts that were racing through my brain, tussling and competing with each other for attention.

'You know I have to do this, don't you?'

And as much as I wanted to rage and scream and kick, I nodded. I knew. This was the mission. This was what we'd risked everything for. This is what everyone had suffered and died for. This was why our parents were locked up somewhere. If this was the only way to test the upload, then he didn't have a choice. I know I'd have done the same.

Mina, Raf and me headed to Surveillance together. No one else. I'd insisted, barring Jack's dad's path when he'd tried to follow us. I didn't want Raf freaked out. Watched like some experiment. Raf sat in a chair in the centre of the room and Mina picked up a lead that snaked out from a port. I held his hair out of the way as Mina coaxed the lead towards the Node. She was about to insert it when Raf put up his hand to stop her.

'Please could you give us a minute, Mina?'

Mina nodded and tactfully withdrew to the other end of the room.

Raf squeezed my hand tight and looked up into my eyes.

'Listen to me for a minute, Noa. No interruptions. No jokes, OK? I love you. I think I always will. We've had our issues and I won't say you haven't really hurt me. I'm still hurting. But, I love you and I need you to know that … just in case, you know…'

'I love you, too,' I replied instantly, blinking back tears, trying to remain strong for him. And it wasn't a lie. As the words escaped my mouth I could feel the truth in them. This boy was special to me in a way no one else could ever be. It wasn't that he'd replaced Jack in my heart; it was like they'd always occupied different parts. Atria and ventricles. Love and friendship.

'But you can tell me again after this thing, OK? Nothing's going to go wrong. Tell me again in five minutes, OK?'

Raf nodded, and Mina took this as her prompt to return and pick up the lead again.

'I still can't see properly, Noa!' she barked.

I adjusted my grip, sweeping more of his hair away from his neck and pressing it against his right ear as Mina squinted and adjusted. Finally, the lead clicked into place.

I'd seen horrific Charles, my mum's boss's son, upload once when we'd done homework together. And I'd seen Raf pretend to upload that time in the library to fool Ms Jones. But neither experience had prepared me for this. I'd cared more about my arm hair than Charles and with Raf I'd watched through an internal window, the glass providing a measure of distance. This time there was no distance. And I cared. I cared so much.

Nothing happened for the first few seconds and just as I was beginning to think it wasn't working, that something had gone wrong, Raf's eyes rolled back in their sockets, red veined white replacing blue and green discs, shuttering his soul. My stomach fell away and I wanted to run out the room, be anywhere but here, but knew I couldn't. This wasn't about me, this was about being there for him, so I ignored my irregular heartbeat, squeezing his hand tighter to let him know I was still there. Slowly at first, and then progressively faster, Raf started to shake. Twitches to shudders to jerks. A jester's marotte. His lips were moving but no sound was coming out. An epileptic attack on mute. I wanted to yank out the lead, to end it, but Mina, seeing the look on my face, scowled me into submission. So I squeezed and blocked and listened to the clitter clatter, clitter clatter as the legs of his chair tap-danced in time to his movements.

The end was abrupt. Dancing to still in a millisecond. A beat and then his eyes rolled back down and stayed there, open but unseeing.

'Raf!' I gasped. 'Raf, are you OK?'

Two beats. And then he blinked.

'Oh God! Oh thank God!' I cried, tears springing from my eyes like mini fountains.

'That … that was strange,' he said slowly, his words initially slurred then becoming clearer. He seemed tired, worn out, but still Raf. My Raf.

'Did it work?' I asked.

'I don't know,' he said carefully. 'Test me on something.'

Mina handed me a sheet of facts they'd put in the upload.

'What is the Avogadro constant?'

'The number of constituent particles contained in a mole of a substance, namely 6×10^{23},' Raf replied without hesitation and then looked totally freaked out. 'That's weird. That's really weird – just suddenly knowing stuff. Having things, information, just inserted into your brain!'

'Does that fact feel any different at all?' I asked, fascinated, wondering if the uploaded information could be like cuckoo eggs, distinguishable from the real deal on close inspection.

'No, no, it's the same. Just the same. God, you can see

why they'd all change and be so mean. There'd be no way of them telling that their opinions had been altered. That these thoughts weren't their own.'

'What about the information about the Ministry brainwashing kids?' Mina asked, impatient to see if the real objective of the upload had succeeded.

Raf thought for a minute, rooting around in his brain for any new information.

'I don't know. I'm definitely very aware of the brainwashing but I already knew that anyway so I can't tell. But I guess if the first bit worked, that probably went in too.'

'So it works! It's going to work!' I exclaimed, jigging around the room. Move over chair legs, there's a new dancer in town.

'Maybe we could get you a better dancing-style upload too?' Raf flashed me a full on wolf grin and I burst out laughing. Laughing like I'd heard the world's funniest-ever joke. Laughing until my eyes returned to his face. Until I saw the two trails of blood winding their way from his nose to his chin.

'LEE!' I screamed. 'Mina, get Lee in here now!'

Raf reached up, felt the trails and stared down at blood-stained fingers.

'It's noth…'

He collapsed mid-word. Sliding off his chair on to the floor. Eyes shut. Lights out.

Lee arrived within seconds. He left Raf on the floor, saying it'd be more dangerous to try to move him, and examined him there.

Fragments of information were thrown in my direction.

Still breathing.

Faint but discernible pulse.

Possible brain haemorrhage.

'Do something!' I screamed. 'Someone's got to do something!'

Lee turned to face me and spoke calmly, ever so calmly. He was no longer my friend. He was a doctor talking to the patient's partner.

'There is nothing I can do for him, Noa. It seems that whatever has been causing his headaches and mood swings, whether it be a shard of bone or internal bleeding and swelling applying pressure, has now worsened, possibly as a result of the upload or possibly coincidentally and his brain tissue may now be ruptured and bleeding. On the other hand, it may be less severe, more localised. The only way to tell would be through an operation.'

'Then we take him to the most skilled brain surgeon,' I said.

'You know we can't,' Lee's tone was patient but tired.

'We can't give up on him. Can't you see that? We've

murdered him. By plugging that lead into his head, we've murdered him! I don't care what you do. I don't care what anyone else does. You can pack up. Clear out of here and move on before it's too late. But, I'm taking him to the Ministry and I'm going hand myself in in return for them operating on Raf and letting my parents go free!' My whole body was trembling now and I felt cold all over.

'Noa,' Jack's voice this time. He'd been drawn, like everyone else, to the noise. 'You can't do this. They'll kill you. They've sent police out to hunt you, for God's sake. They won't operate, they won't let your parents go, you've got nothing to trade with them, nothing that they want.'

'He's right,' Lee again. 'The best thing you can do for him is to hold him, keep talking to him. Make this time, his passing as calm as you can.'

Passing. *Passing*! He made it sound like Raf was going to move into the next room or something. You pass a friend in the street. You pass someone a fork. This wasn't passing. This was death. *Making it calm* was giving up. It was like saying – hey that kid's fallen into some rapids, can you sing a lullaby to it while it drowns? I'm not a singer. To be fair I'm not much of a swimmer either. But I'm damn sure that I'd be jumping into the water after it.

I stared at Raf's body, working out how I was going to get him to the Ministry. I couldn't carry him. Maybe I could sort of prop him up over my shoulder and drag him there?

My thoughts were interrupted by a small voice from the corner.

'There is something they'd want.'

I turned round to see the speaker – Nell – looking scared and vulnerable, yet determined at the same time. 'Something you can trade,' she continued.

'What?' I snapped. I didn't have time to waste. Every second spent talking was a second Raf was away from a surgeon.

'Me,' came the reply.

I was so mad with anger and fear that I almost bit Nell's head off.

'What are you talking about? Why on earth would they want you?'

Nell flinched as if ducking the words, but stood her ground.

'I've been thinking about it for a while,' she answered. 'Ever since you talked about splicing – you know about what genes are and how they determine something's characteristics and how they put genes from one thing into another when they make the Mucor bars?'

I nodded, remembering all the times I'd caught her staring at a Mucor bar packet, lost in thought.

'Well, I must have a different gene, mustn't I? Look at me!' she tugged at her white blonde hair and pointed to her ghostly skin. 'And I don't get malaria. I don't get ill. I could survive in the Wetlands. Others can't, but I can. So maybe, maybe they could take my genes and splice them into normal people. Then lots of people could live out there. It wouldn't be the greatest place, but it'd be a life. More people could live.'

I stared at her, open-mouthed. She was right, she was completely right. How I'd underestimated this girl.

'But surely the Ministry already know about Cells?' Jasmine chimed in. Even here, in the Opposition headquarters, the Ministry was regarded as all seeing, all knowing.

'No,' I replied. 'No, they wouldn't. They never go into the Wetlands, do they? They drop prisoners off, bomb the region next to the Fence and occasionally retrieve a crashed satellite, but they never patrol, never visit the settlements. I don't think they have any idea.'

'Hold on a minute,' Jack broke in quickly. 'We're not handing Nell over to be experimented on.' He'd always been protective of Nell, father-like. Memories of the beds in the Laboratory that Raf and me had discovered assaulted me. Children lying there, tubes in their arms, charts above their heads. Jack was right. We couldn't just hand her over to have that happen to her. Nell's genes might be able to save thousands of lives, maybe tens of thousands, but in the end the Ministry was kind of right in a way. Not every life is equal. It should be, but it isn't. The Ministry prioritise money. But I couldn't help but prioritise too. The lives of your friends and family have more weight. The concept of balance, of utilitarianism, doesn't apply to them.

'We wouldn't need to hand her over.' Lee spoke slowly, deep in thought. 'They don't need her to see that you're telling the truth. They just need her DNA. All we need is a couple of hairs and a photo.'

'They'll just take the hairs and kill you,' Jack's voice was raised now, raised and angry. 'We need to think this through!'

'There's no time!' I yelled back. 'They'll need me alive as they'll want to find Nell, examine her. Raf can't wait. He'll die if I wait any longer. And, have you forgotten, but we've got two dead policemen in the next room? People are going to come looking for them. Soon. Time is not a luxury we have.'

Jack was going to speak again but his dad silenced him with a glance.

'Noa's right. Go. Now.'

'The upload?' I asked.

'We'll take care of it.'

'And Nell?'

'She'll come with us. We know how to disappear.'

'Be careful,' Mina warned as we left. 'You're going to

give them this important, world-changing information about this new gene and you're not going to have any witnesses. No one apart from us to know what you're offering them. No one to ensure that you walk out safe at the end.'

'We'll be OK,' I said, more forcefully than I felt. 'They can't turn this down. Not something like this. And we've walked away before. We'll walk away again.'

The van screeched round the corner and then Milk Teeth slammed on the brakes.

'Careful!' I yelled. 'His head!' But we were already at a standstill directly in front of the Ministry building.

Jack kicked open the back doors and we jumped out, Raf supported on a stretcher between us, Nell's hair and the Polaroid Lee had quickly taken of her securely zipped into my jacket pocket. Jack's dad hadn't wanted Jack to go. Had forbidden it in fact. But it was obvious Jack wasn't going to listen to him. So Jack's dad had done the only other thing he could think of. Provided us with back-up.

Already police were swarming down the steps towards us. We'd encroached on hallowed ground. We were in an unmarked van in a pedestrianised zone. We were clearly trouble. Milk Teeth and gang leapt from the van, too, and threw themselves into the police's path. Attracting their attention, drawing their batons towards them like iron nails to a magnet. I saw Milk Teeth, fighting back before disappearing under a bonfire of flailing arms. Guilt hit me. I'd hated this guy. Thought him unbearably cruel, bordering on psychopathic, but in the end he'd had his own morality. He wasn't just on a power trip. He was a believer. Ready to die for the cause.

'Come on!' Jack hissed. We scuttled past the fray and up the steps, trying to keep the stretcher as steady as possible, acutely aware of each bump and jolt as we ran.

Just four more steps to go.

Three.

Two.

'Stop!'

A policeman blocked our path. Separate from the pack. He must have emerged later from the building. Tall anyway, the two-step advantage he had over us conferred on him giant status.

'This is Ministry property. You have no right to be here.'

He grabbed my arm and lifted his baton. Verbal persuasion clearly wasn't his thing.

'Wait!' I shouted. 'Don't you recognise my face?'

The sun was in his eyes so he had to squint to focus on my features. Once he'd figured it out, the squint was replaced by the beginnings of a lazy grin.

'Noa Blake,' he declared. 'Well, well, well. We've been looking for you.'

'I'm here to trade information.'

'I see.' The policeman could still barely conceal his smile. *Denser*, it said. *Gullible Denser*. 'And these are?' he included Jack and Raf in a contemptuous hand circle.

'They're with me,' I replied before Jack could say anything. 'Their safety is part of the deal. We need a doctor now. A brain surgeon. Or I don't say anything.'

'Tell that to a minister,' the policeman replied, his lips twitching. 'I'm sure they'll be very interested.' And he escorted us to the heavy entrance doors, never once letting go of my arm. He wanted to claim credit for my capture. Maybe he had kids or there was a reward or promotion at stake.

He dragged us through the hall, waving away attempts by anyone else at assistance, and into an elevator. I silently thanked Lee for having strapped Raf in as we had to tilt the stretcher to make it fit. I scanned the board detailing the occupancies of the different floors. First Floor was marked P. Khan: Minister for Food and E. Scott: Minister for Education, Second floor was J. Cartwright: Minister for Allocation and G. Riley: Minister for Health. The list went on. Five floors of Ministers. Which would he press?

None of the above.

His finger hit B for basement and the lift started its descent. My stomach dropped. I'd learnt by now that basements were never good.

'I need to speak to a minister now!' I said, trying to sound authoritative but failing, and hating the sound of desperation I could hear seeping into my voice. 'We need the operation now!'

'All in good time,' the policeman replied.

'We don't have time,' Jack snapped back, unprepared to act as silent sidekick any longer. 'Our friend is going to die if he's not seen immediately. And if he dies we don't tell you. We have information that would save tens of thousands, maybe hundreds of thousands of lives, and we'll be sure to tell whoever's in charge that it's you who's at fault. You who messed it all up.'

The policeman didn't respond. We reached the basement and the lift doors opened with a ping. My ribcage stopped working, froze. I was back in the ice tunnel of my nightmare. Shards filling my throat. I readied myself to follow him. To head down to some lightless torture chamber. I'd failed Raf. I'd failed Jack. I'd failed my parents. My vision had been right. Everyone I come into contact with dies.

But something in Jack's words must have struck a chord with the policeman. The spectre of blame had appeared before him with an outstretched finger. Apart from a tiny shake of his head, he didn't move. Didn't leave the lift. Instead, his finger found the glowing 2 button and we were moving again. Ascending.

It was the Minister for Allocation's door that the policeman knocked on. Or rather opened mid-knock, not bothering to wait for a 'come in'.

'What the…'

J. Cartwright clearly wasn't used to being interrupted mid-afternoon and certainly not by a policeman and three teenagers, two conscious, one less so.

He was exactly as he appeared on TV. A small man, neat grey hair and rectangular black-framed glasses. He looked like all the other lawyers in Dad's office. Someone plucked from a vat of indistinguishable lawyer/accountant waxworks and then animated. He was staring at a screen of figures and surrounded by a nest of files. Order was his friend. Probably his only one.

He made to turf us out of the room and call security when the policeman explained that we supposedly had information. Important information.

'It's Noa Blake,' he added. 'I've brought her in.'

'Noa Blake?'

The Minister looked at me properly for the first time. Studied me. Eyes all aglow behind the frames. Like I was some particularly rare species of butterfly that he'd discovered and was going to admire before mounting on a board with a pin.

'Now tell me, did you actually go to the Wetlands and come back again?'

'Yes, that's me,' I replied, trying to look tough, channelling Milk Teeth. Everything was riding on this. On me.

'So, where did you catch her?' he asked the policeman.

'Um.'

'On the steps,' I replied before the policeman could invent some malc story that made him look massively heroic. 'I came voluntarily. I have information to trade in exchange for an operation for my friend and the release of my parents.'

'Is that right?' The Minister looked at me, frowned and then removed his glasses to clean them, rubbing them with a blue cloth he took out of his trouser pocket. To give him a better look at the specimen in front of him. He seemed almost sad. Like he knew my coming here had doomed me, that they were going to kill me and he didn't want them to. Not that he was going to stop them. Even though he worked in allocation, people were probably just numbers to him, pawns to be moved round a board. Life and death didn't touch him first hand. I fought down the fear that was expanding and rising in my stomach, spreading in convection currents through the rest of my body. Told myself that he didn't know what information I had. How game-changing it was.

'There's a gene,' I said, forcing myself to keep going before the fear that had frozen my face reached my vocal chords. 'A gene that's arisen in the Wetlands that confers immunity to malaria. If we add that gene to future children, a whole new generation can safely colonise the Wetlands. We can do away with the TAA. We can save thousands and thousands of lives!'

As I spoke, I unzipped my jacket pocket and held out the photo of Nell for him to see. Her whiteness radiated off the paper. New. Alien. A different species almost.

Instantly, the sadness evaporated from the Minister's face. Instead he was almost salivating from curiosity, his brain already shuffling numbers, allocating citizens.

'This is incredible,' he said. 'I'd always wondered whether this might happen. Humans adapting to their environment. Genetic mutations arising, giving an adaptive advantage. Fascinating. Totally fascinating. And the practical implications … oh my.'

He was almost rubbing his hands with glee and I started to relax. Let some of the tension go from my face. They realised the importance of the gene. It would change society.

'Where's the girl now? I need to see the girl.'

OK. Time for the negotiations to commence.

'You don't see her until my friend is operated on and my parents' release is guaranteed. Not until we all walk out of here alive.' The tremor had left my voice and my face could have won a poker tournament. This was as high stakes as it could get and I was going all in.

'You know they can make you talk?' He was whispering now. Almost like he didn't want anyone to overhear. 'Give up the girl's location. Please. It's not a betrayal. Everyone talks in the end. The things they do...' His voice trailed off and he began to clean his glasses again, like it was some tic he'd developed when he approached the outskirts of any emotion.

'I don't actually think they can.' A calm fell over me and I felt the truth of my words. 'You've already hurt every person I love. I don't think there's anything else left for you to do to me.'

The Minister stood and looked at me and I watched our power reverse. He saw the determination in my face and was scared. Probably for the first time in his life. He was scared that he was going to miss out on this opportunity. One more push was all that was needed.

'You can test her DNA though.' I handed over the three hairs Lee had plucked from Nell's head. 'Run it and you'll see a new gene there, one no one's seen before.'

His child-size hand, cradled the phone, hesitated and then picked it up.

Make the call, I prayed. Please, please make the call.

'I need a DNA test ... expedited ... now means now.'

Without even looking up at me, he hung up and made another call.

'I need an ambulance, now. Yes. The Ministry... And notify your best surgeon. He's needed.'

It was like someone had liquefied all the bones in my body, reducing me to a jellied mass of unsupported flesh and blood. I'd done it. They were going to operate on Raf. They were going to save him!

The ambulance men arrived within minutes and Raf was carried away. I started to go with him when the Minister stopped me.

'No, not you. I know you're worried about your friend, but the best thing that you can do for him right now is to stay here. Show that you're cooperative. Pliant.' His voice was kindly, even if I didn't like the words that accompanied it. Pliant? *Pliant?*

'Jack, you go,' I urged, but Jack shook his head.

'I'm staying with you. Raf's unconscious. He doesn't need me.'

I wanted to scream at him, but I knew it was pointless. And anyway, if it was all a trick, if they were just pretending to operate, what exactly could Jack do? He couldn't take out the whole of the Ministry's security. He'd just end up dead too.

'Don't move, either of you. Please.' With that instruction, the Minister left the room, ordering the policeman who was still lingering around outside, no doubt waiting for his reward, to guard the door.

There was only one chair in the room, the Minister's leather swivel chair by his desk. It felt contaminated somehow, like particles of the Ministry and everything it stood for were still hovering next to it, fog clinging to a hillside. Neither of us wanted to touch it, let alone sit in it, so instead we sat on the floor, leaning against each other as a side support. We weren't really talking. It was too serious for that. We just sat and stared at the clock, watching the minutes tick by. Waiting for news about the DNA. About Raf. Two o'clock became half past two became three o'clock, still with no sign of the Minister.

I must have fallen asleep as the next thing I knew, Jack was nudging me awake.

'Look!' he was exclaiming, pointing wildly at the clock. 'Look!' I followed his finger and gazed at the round face and black arms.

'What?' I didn't get it.

'It's four-thirty, Noa!'

'So?'

'The upload! It'll be sitting in Scribes, ready. Right now Childes everywhere will learning the truth, discovering that they've been systematically brainwashed by the Ministry.'

'If your dad's held out long enough. If they've managed to transmit it.'

'They'll have done it, Noa. I know they will.'

He had such faith and I envied him for a moment until realised that I felt it too. Knew it too. They'd have managed it. Whatever it took.

We just sat there, letting the enormity of it sink in.

Upwards of two hundred thousand kids having their lives turned upside down. Questioning the extent to which their thoughts and opinions were or ever had been their own.

'I can't imagine it, finding out that your life has been a lie,' I said at last.

'I can,' Jack replied sadly.

'How do you think they're going to feel?'

'Angry. Really, really angry.'

No one came for us and afternoon drifted into evening. At about eight, the door was opened and a tray with some bread and Mucor bake was pushed inside.

'What's going on?' I asked the retreating hand. But no response followed and the door was shut with a clunk and then locked.

The lights went out at around nine. Well, they switched into motion-detector mode to conserve energy so the only way to see was to jump up and wiggle your arms about. It was funny at first but soon lost its humour. We spent the night huddled together for comfort, trying to block out the not knowing. Not knowing if Raf had made it. Not knowing how the other ministers were reacting to the news of the gene. Not knowing if anyone had told my parents I was here. Not knowing if there were any plans to let us go.

It was morning when we were finally fetched. It wasn't the Minister, it was three guys and two girls in black uniform who dragged us up to standing and ordered us to follow them. They carried guns, tasers and batons. Refusal wasn't an option.

'Ministry bodyguards,' Jack hissed in my ear. This was serious. Properly serious. The bodyguards only accompanied the Head Minister. We'd come to the attention of the big fish in the pond. The shark.

They surrounded us, a rugby scrum in which we were the ball, ready to be hooked and pummelled.

'What's going on?' I asked.

No response. Silently, we were marched to the far side of the building, to a different lift from the one we'd used before. Bundled inside, one of the guards inserted a key into a lock below the buttons, turned it and pressed level six. The other lift didn't have a level six. My head was scrambling so I focused on my breathing.

IN – it's natural that the Head Minister would be interested in this new gene – AND OUT– of course he's going to want to question me – AND IN – oh God oh GOD! – AND OUT – it's going to be OK. It's all going to be OK.

The lift doors opened and we exited into a penthouse suite. Gone were the glass-walled office cubicles and admin staff. Gone was the occasional semi-dehydrated pot plant and water fountain. Here we were in luxury. Open-planned, wood-panelled luxury with a sideboard of breakfast snacks that weren't Mucor or parsnip-based. A large dark wood table stood in the middle of the room, round which sat the ten Ministers – seven men, three women – some of whom I recognised from TV broadcasts, some of whom I didn't. All well fed, well groomed, well dressed. Rationing, poverty, struggle, these were abstract concepts up here. To be read about rather than experienced. I acknowledged the Minister for Allocation at the end of one side but my eyes only rested momentarily on him before being pulled towards the head of the table. For there, in a chair marked out as more important by its arms and larger size, was the Head Minister. Tall, even more imposing in real life. I was five metres away from the most powerful person in the Territory.

Emotions fought for control of my head. Acute, bladder-squeezing terror wrestled with pure muscle-clenching anger. This was the face of our enemy. The face of the system that had killed my friends, sent children to their deaths and taken my parents. This was the face I wanted to claw to shreds, the green eyes I wanted to close forever.

'So, Noa,' the Head Minister stood up and walked towards us, circling us before coming to a standstill, his back to the window, king of his domain. His voice was soft, intentionally so. So that you had to lean in towards him to listen, a snake drawing its prey closer so they're easier to eat. 'It does indeed seem that you've stumbled across a new gene.'

Yes! My chest opened, my breath moved more easily. It didn't matter that it had taken all night – we'd convinced them.

He continued, raising his voice slightly. There was a growing buzz from outside, presumably down on the street and he needed to project to drown it out.

'Obviously without the test subject present to examine, we can only take your word for the fact that this gene does indeed confer malarial immunity.'

'It does. It really does,' Jack broke in, only to be silenced by a glare and a raised hand.

'So, it raises interesting possibilities.'

We'd done it. We'd done it. The TAA would end. The whole Childe programme would cease. The Fence would fall.

'But,' he continued, 'on reflection we have decided not to pursue them.'

What? His words were a punch to the face. The sort that knocks out teeth and breaks noses. Not pursue them? Not pursue the chance to save thousands and thousands of lives? I stared at the faces of the other Ministers. No one met my eye. The Minister of Allocation stood up to speak but was pulled down by the minister next to him and silenced.

The Head Minister continued. 'We believe that a life in the Wetlands, even without the risk of malaria, is not one which we should offer to our citizens. It is preferable to maintain the status quo, whereby the brightest citizens remain within the Territory and the less desirable are removed. This is the best chance for the long-term success of our nation.'

Every word was a pin in a voodoo doll. Piercing my organs, stabbing at my heart. I should have anticipated it but it had never once crossed my mind that they wouldn't do the right thing. That they didn't care. Didn't care about ordinary people at all. As long as they and their cronies were safe, everyone else could go to hell. Heaven forbid one of their offspring or grandchildren should be given immunity and allocated to the Wetlands. Heaven forbid they should stop the Childe programme and end total freakoid obedience or have their friends' food rations slightly reduced to make way for a larger population.

Without a flicker of emotion, the Head Minister continued. 'You will now reveal the whereabouts of this girl to us as we obviously don't want her ... differences ... to become common knowledge.'

'Go to hell!' I yelled at him. 'I'm not going to tell you anything. You can torture me, kill me, I don't care. You don't get her! She's a twelve-year-old girl, for God's sake. Leave her alone!'

The Head Minister laughed. Well, he opened his mouth and a *ha ha* sound came out, but there was no merriment to it. No joy.

'I'm not going to torture you, Noa. Or kill you for that matter. I like your brain too much.'

I should have felt relief, but I didn't. There was something about his voice, his eyes that signalled this wasn't a reprieve. He wasn't handing me a *get out of jail free* card.

'You've shown yourself to be resourceful, inventive. It'd be a waste to kill you. We need minds like yours in the Territory.'

'I'm not going to work for you,' I spat. 'I'd never work for you!'

'And therein lies the problem. We want your mind, just a slightly more pliant and obedient version.'

Pliant. That word again. He paused and the silence turned static.

'You've been scheduled for a late upgrade this evening.'

'NO!' I screamed, my shout immediately echoed by Jack's roar. 'NO! You can't. You can't do this to us!' Jack had balled his hands into a fist and leapt forward to hulk bash him. Two guards intercepted the blow and Jack's legs were kicked out beneath him.

'No, no,' the Head Minister smiled cruelly. 'You mistake

me. There's no "us". You, Noa Blake, will have an upgrade. The best surgeon, mind you, no expense spared. You, Jack Munro – yes, we know who you are – you're, how shall I put it tactfully … less obviously valuable.'

'What are you going to do to him?' I shouted.

But the Head Minister didn't answer. He'd already turned his back on us, redirecting his attention to the street below, staring through the glass double doors and over the low wall of the balcony beyond. We were forgotten to him. Mere details, crossed off his to-do list.

'I'll remember!' I yelled at the back of his head, as the guards took hold of my arms. 'I'll remember and tell everyone.'

The Head Minister didn't even bother to turn round.

'No, no, you won't,' he laughed. 'Take them away.'

As we were being dragged back towards the lift, he couldn't resist one parting shot.

'Oh, and your other friend. He made it by the way. He's already got a Node so we'll probably just reprogramme him too. So you won't be alone in your new life. It'll be just like old times.'

Every step we took towards the lift was like a nail being hammered into a coffin. They were going to kill Jack. Jack and my parents would be dead. No more. Dust and bone. And me, it was almost worse. I'd still exist, in body anyway, but my mind, my mind would be theirs. To work in their name. I'd be reprogrammed to revere the Ministry. Maybe they'd even design an upload specially. Tailor-made just for me. They'd change my thoughts, my beliefs. Everything precious, everything that mattered to me would be erased. Gone. Would I even remember Jack and Mum and Dad or would they remove all trace of them? Would they make me think they were traitors? Their deaths deserved? The blood started to pound in my ears, *boom boom boom.*

Think positive, Mum used to say. When the world seems to be crushing you, think of one positive thing and focus on that, keep it in your mind's eye and then amplify it, expand it so it fills your whole field of vision and then, for that moment, there's nothing bad left to worry about. I tried to think about getting to spend my last few moments with Jack. About how lucky I was to have a friend who cared this much for me, who'd risked his life over and over to keep me safe. I tried to think of Raf. About the fact that he'd survived the operation. That I'd get to see him again. But the images never stuck. They'd expand and then pop like a balloon on a pin and be replaced with visions of my parents, thin, broken, dying, and images, flashes of what waited below.

'Jesus!' A shout broke into my thoughts.

The lift doors were an open mouth but no one was pushing us forward. The Ministers, the guards, everyone's focus had been pulled elsewhere. To the newly opened balcony door where the Head Minister stood. To the sight and sounds of the street.

Me and Jack used the distraction to head over there ourselves. To see what the stress was about.

My eyes couldn't quite absorb it all so they blinked, refocused and blinked again. There, six floors below us, the street was a mass of people. People as far as the eye could see. People swarming up the steps, people balancing on bollards, people holding up placards and shouting. Shouting at the top of their lungs.

'Jasmine's work?' I whispered to Jack, awed.

'I don't know,' he whispered back. 'She's never managed something this big before. Nothing on this scale.'

I scanned the tiny faces and my heart's rhythm went all experimental jazz. Two faces made it stop beating altogether.

'Look there!' I instructed Jack. 'To the left of the stop sign. Isn't that Hugo?'

Jack squinted through the window, straining his eyes. 'You're right,' he said slowly. 'And that looks like Charles to his left!'

Freakoids.

Childes had joined in a demonstration against the Ministry. For the first time ever. The Ministry's hold was crumbling. Our upload must have worked! Then I started to read the hastily made placards, to really listen to the chants.

Use the Gene
Stop your Lies
Colonise the Wetlands
Uploads are Evil
Cells are the Future
Let Noa and Jack go!

It wasn't Jasmine. It was Mina. Mina who'd been so desperately worried that we wouldn't have any witnesses. Mina who'd created two hundred thousand witnesses of her own.

'She changed the upload!' I crowed, not bothering to whisper anymore. 'She added information about the gene, about our sharing it with the Ministry!'

The Head Minister swivelled round and stared at me, eyes flashing.

'What have you done?'

A radio transmitter was produced and commands were being fired down it to the police patrols and army squadrons that were arriving at the scene.

'Disperse the crowds!'

'Break them up!'

But the numbers were too great. The concentrated mass of protestors, bodies, both a weapon and a shield.

'They know,' I said, calmly and clearly. 'They know you've been brainwashing them. They know about the gene. They're not just going to go home this time.'

The other Ministers had joined the Head Minister by the window and they were desperately discussing strategy.

'We need to mow them down. Send a message,' the Head Minister was urging.

'I agree. Open fire,' from the weasely Minister for Communication.

But other faces were more wary. Uncomfortable.

'No.' To my surprise the Minister of Allocation refused to be silenced this time and his voice had stolen some authority, borrowed a measure of passion. 'If we kill this number of people, the Ministry is over. There will be a full-scale rebellion. Their friends. Their parents. We'll be back to the dark days of in-fighting and war. And look at us? This isn't why we went into governance. Remember? We formed this government to end the violence. We wanted to provide a better life. There were harsh choices. But the original aim was to do good. To restore order. To save our country.'

'You always were too squeamish,' the Head Minister retorted. 'Never fully behind the Childe programme. Critical of the TAA. Just because you don't have children.

Have nothing to protect. And what do you suggest we do then? Lay down a red carpet and welcome them inside?' The Head Minister's tone was icy.

'We do what we've always done,' the Minister for Allocation replied, matching him ice for ice. 'We control the situation. Fire one shot and you've lost control. Forever.'

Another radio report crackled in.

'They're approaching the doors. They've broken through the first police cordon.'

The Head Minister stared at the transmitter and we waited, shoulders hunched to our ears. Waited for him to give the order. Waited for the massacre to come.

One-Mississippi. Two-Mississippi.

'Bring me a megaphone,' he barked. 'We're going outside.'

A minion scuttled off and returned with one. Then, plastering on his best 1000-watt smile, the Head Minister grabbed my arm and Jack's and pushed the balcony door fully open, dragging us outside with him.

The megaphone squealed into life and thousands of heads swivelled to watch us.

'Greetings fellow citizens!' boomed out the Head Minister's voice. Warm, welcoming, you'd have thought he'd called this rally himself and was addressing his supporters. I almost admired his nerve. Almost.

'Thank you for joining us on this most joyful of days!'

What? Where was he going with this?

There was a softer buzz as the crowd was as puzzled as I was. A swarm suddenly stumped as the queen pulls an unexpected U-turn.

'I am here to announce two important new policies that we have had to keep under wraps until now due to security concerns. Firstly, the Childe programme is being decommissioned.' The crowd, quietened, deflated.

'Secondly,' the Head Minister continued quickly, pushing home his advantage, 'thanks to the resolve and ingenuity of my young friends Noa Blake and Jack Munro, here of their own free will I might add, we have at our hands a most wonderful discovery. A gene. Yes, a new gene that confers malarial resistance. That will allow us to colonise the Wetlands and significantly increase our population!' At this point he grabbed one of each of our hands and held them aloft in a kind of victory salute. He was linking us to him. Gaining credit. Crushing resistance.

A beat and then the crowd let out a roar of approval.

'What's going on?' I whispered to Jack.

'They're forgiving him,' he replied, furious. 'They're letting him get away with it. Dad always said people like to be governed. They like strong leadership. As long as certain lines aren't crossed. And he's just stepped back from that line.'

I nodded. I got it. No one wants full-on rebellion, civil war. So many people would die. So many lives wasted. He'd given people a way out. Reform rather than revolt.

But we couldn't trust them to follow through. Couldn't leave our fate in their hands. The protestors would go home. The moment would pass. But what was there to guarantee that the Ministry would actually use the gene? What was to stop them pretending to trial it and then declaring it ineffective? And what about our security – mine, Jack's, Raf's, Mum's, Dad's? What would happen as soon as those balcony doors closed again? I had to act.

Summoning every last reserve of energy, I snatched the megaphone from the Head Minister's hands.

'What are you doing?' asked a startled Jack.

'Controlling the situation,' I replied.

Clearing my voice, I started to speak.

'I'd like to thank everyone for coming here today too. You are our witnesses. It is you, the people, who will hold us accountable on our promises.' Another roar of approval. The Head Minister tried to grab the megaphone again, but I sidestepped out of his reach and he couldn't tackle me to the floor without shattering the pretence of friendship.

'And I have another couple of announcements to make.'

'Stop it now!' hissed the Head Minister, through a strained smile, but I just smiled back at him, matching him watt for watt.

'My mother, Rachel Blake, an eminent scientist at the Laboratory will be heading up the gene programme and providing weekly televised reports to citizens on her progress.' *Try and kill her or Dad now!* 'And Jack, Raf and

I will be assisting her at a much lower level. We will all be leaving the building in half an hour to meet people in person and answer any questions you might have.'

'Don't think you'll survive this,' the Head Minister whispered, all trace of a smile now gone. My stomach twisted. I thought I'd been so clever, but he was right. We might get out the building, but another day, maybe not tomorrow but one day, he'd send his bodyguards after us. And that day we wouldn't wake up.

He lunged for the megaphone again, but I managed to keep hold of it. Time for one final announcement.

'And, saving the most important till last,' I said, addressing the crowds below, hearing my voice bounce from street to street. 'I would like to thank the Head Minister for his years of dedicated service to the Territory as it is with great sadness that I announce that this will be his last day in office. He has decided to step down to spend more time with his family. Our new leader will be Mr Cartwright, previously the Minister for Allocation. So it's both goodbye and welcome.'

The Head Minister found my right wrist and was pushing it back, grabbing at the megaphone. Pain seared up my arm. The bones were going to snap. I screamed as he wrenched it from my grasp.

'Wait…' he began. But no one could hear him. The roar of approval at his replacement was so loud that all his attempts to drown them out failed.

'Fire on them, Fire on them!' he barked into the radio transmitter instead, but the Minister for Allocation stepped forward and snatched that from him.

'Abort order,' he shouted. 'Stand down.'

No shot was fired and the Head Minister seemed to crumple in on himself as he saw his power vanish before him.

Then. Ever so calmly, the Minister for Allocation seized the Head Minister's hand and held it aloft. A forced victory salute. I handed him the megaphone.

'Thank you for your support.' The crowd quietened as they took in their new leader.

'It is time for a change,' his voice rang out. 'And that change starts now.'

He spoke fluently and articulately for a good twenty minutes.

And he didn't rub his glasses once.

Life's now settled into a kind of rhythm. A pattern. Days are spent with Mum at the Laboratory, studying the gene. Making sure we know the exact sequence of base pairs and how to cut it out, splice in and reproduce it using bacterial plasmids. The first human trial is next week. A volunteer. A mum whose son is in the Wetlands and whose guilt at staying behind has eaten her up inside. She'd do anything, try anything to be with him again.

I like working with Mum. Really like it. She's so good at what she does … knowledgeable, in charge and totally calm when a machine breaks down or an emergency button pings. Lots of the time I catch myself looking out for someone else walking by just so I can say, 'See that top super-scientist – that's my mum!'

And finally I can smile when I look at her, too. And Dad. I couldn't for the first few weeks. They were both so thin, gaunt. Mum's hair is now streaked with grey and Dad has lost his completely. Totally bald. Eyebrows gone too. Just a forehead that stretches on and on. Huge stress can do that to you. I cried when I first saw them, when the door to their cell was unlocked and opened. Assaulted by guilt and love and remorse.

'I'm so sorry,' was all I could splutter between sobs. 'I'm so, so sorry.' And they ended up comforting me as if I had been the one caged and tortured, the one abandoned and betrayed.

'It's OK, Noa bean,' Mum murmured as she stroked my hair. 'You're safe and that's all we care about. That's all we've ever cared about.'

They've never told me exactly what happened to them and I don't think they ever will. It's like a chapter of their lives has been torn out and burnt. Only to be revived, phoenix-like, at night, in their dreams.

Outwardly, they've recovered quickly though. Extra rations, rest, every luxury to get Mum looking presentable for her first televised progress update. We've been given a new flat too. It's larger than before, with four bedrooms instead of two. It seems a bit like blood money, but we're not in a position to turn it down and the extra rooms have been filled quickly enough anyway as Jack and Nell have moved in. Nell obviously had no family of her own in the Territory and Jack, well Jack couldn't face going back to his mum's, and his dad's wasn't exactly an option. His dad has disappeared again, despite being officially pardoned. We went to the building, the Opposition headquarters, and it'd been totally cleared out. The bodies of the policemen had gone. There wasn't any sign of a struggle, no blood-spattered walls or anything, so they must have got out straight after transmitting the upload.

A parcel turned up yesterday from Jack's dad. The note inside apologising for leaving again but saying how important it was that the Opposition kept going, that someone kept watch over the new Head Minister, to stop history repeating itself. I expected Jack to be hurt again, angry again, but he seemed to be at peace with it. Wrapped inside the note was an illegal mobile phone with a sticker saying 'speed dial 1' attached. This time his dad hadn't just walked away. Contact hadn't been severed and Jack knew, understood that he was still special. His dad's way of protecting him, being there for him, was being away.

Most of my evenings are spent with Raf. He's doing really well. The doctors said full recovery could take three to six months, but the dizziness is mainly gone. The mood swings over. And we don't have to hide anymore. We can wander the streets together, hand in hand, cap-free. A Norm and a freakoid in a new world that's finding its way.

Change isn't instantaneous. It's not like you make a speech, swap a leader and suddenly the water recedes, an endless supply of manna drops from heaven and everyone dances around together. The Fence hasn't fallen yet. It'll stand, its mosquito grids in place until malarial resistance has been achieved for every citizen. But the TAA won't take place this year. And the Childe production facility has been closed. Changes that I'd always dreamt of, but never thought I'd see.

The biggest difference though is in the atmosphere. The feel of the place. Fear has a smell. A stultifying effect. It dulls and hunches and leaches energy. That's gone, replaced by a new fragrance: hope. It's like it's spring even though it's actually mid-December.

Last night me and Raf had a picnic in the park. He'd brought a rug and we lay out on it, hours after sundown, talking, eating, just being there, savouring the evening and each other.

'Annie from the Peak was right,' Raf said at one point, rolling over so that his head blocked my view of the midnight sky, white teeth replacing silver stars. 'We should never give up on humanity.'

'Mmm,' I replied, grinning back. 'But what about wolves? What should we do about them?'

Acknowledgements

Huge thanks again to my husband for his constant encouragement and support. Thanks to Nina for her invaluable feedback on early drafts. Thanks to my agent, Jane Turnbull, for taking on these books with so much passion. Thanks to Penny Thomas at Firefly for being a brilliant editor and to Megan Farr. Thanks to Karolina Davison for being an unstoppable force of nature, really getting my books out there and for supplying the all-important 'jazz hands'. Thanks to Caitlin, Ollie, Tom and all the pupils at Emanuel, Graveney, Ibstock and Waldegrave who helped choose the cover. Thanks to Jerome Smith for talking me through hacking and digital signatures – any errors here are my own. Finally, thanks to my parents for providing emergency childcare during editing sessions.

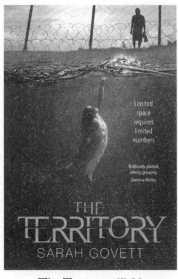

The Territory £7.99
978-1-910080-18-4

The Territory, Escape £7.99
978-1-910080-46-7

'Simply impossible to put down ... the whole
series is a brilliant, five star read.'
Sarah J. Harris